"Why are you really in Hope?" he asked.

She was silent, and for a moment he thought she might not answer. Then she said, "My mom left Hope pregnant and never came back. I never knew my dad, but I'd like to get to know him, if I get the chance."

Her dad... Had she applied for the only job available to buy herself a little more time in town...or did she think *Mr. Harmon* was her father? He had questions, but she was turning away again.

"Good night, Hank," she called softly over her shoulder. "See you at breakfast."

He waited until she got inside before he headed back toward the road. He was jaded from a messy divorce and she was looking for a dad she'd never met. It was the reality check he needed. Attraction was one thing, but he liked to be realistic. He was her boss, and if he let those lines get blurred, he'd lose his job, smear his reputation and find himself back down at the bottom of the heap on another ranch.

Dear Reader,

My husband asked me to marry him after two weeks. We've been married twelve years now, and the other day, I was chattering about something and I said, "But you didn't plan that proposal, right?" He gave me a funny look and said, "Of course I planned it."

And while a two-week romance might sound like a spontaneous thing, he'd walked me to that fountain on that summer night because he wanted to ask me to marry him. And I only *just* figured that out!

As a romance novelist, I'm often asked if my books are "realistic." And I have to say—yes! I write what I believe, and I believe in love that lasts and men who commit. In my humble opinion, forever is not too much to ask for.

If you'd like to connect with me, you can find me on Facebook or at my website, patriciajohnsromance.com.

Patricia Johns

HER COWBOY BOSS

PATRICIA JOHNS

⬦ HARLEQUIN® WESTERN ROMANCE

Recycling programs
for this product may
not exist in your area.

ISBN-13: 978-0-373-75771-8

Her Cowboy Boss

Printed in U.S.A.

www.Harlequin.com

Patricia Johns writes from Alberta, Canada. She has her Hon. BA in English literature and currently writes for Harlequin's Love Inspired, Western Romance and Heartwarming lines. You can find her at patriciajohnsromance.com.

Books by Patricia Johns

Harlequin Western Romance

Hope, Montana

Safe in the Lawman's Arms
Her Stubborn Cowboy
The Cowboy's Christmas Bride
The Cowboy's Valentine Bride
The Triplets' Cowboy Daddy

Harlequin Love Inspired

Comfort Creek Lawmen

Deputy Daddy

His Unexpected Family
The Rancher's City Girl
A Firefighter's Promise
The Lawman's Surprise Family

Harlequin Heartwarming

A Baxter's Redemption
The Runaway Bride

Visit the Author Profile page
at Harlequin.com for more titles.

To my husband—he's the best choice I ever made!

Chapter One

So this is my dad.

Avery Southerly shook Louis Harmon's calloused hand, suppressing a wince at his too-tight grasp. He was in his midforties with a potbelly and a white cowboy hat that shaded his heat-reddened face. His dark eyes were kind, and he gave her a cordial nod. He'd only have been nineteen when she was born, but somehow, she'd always imagined her father looking older than this.

With a quick look around the property, she could tell that he ran a clean ranch. The front yard had been recently mowed, and the drive was clear of vehicles. The fence that separated yard from pasture was well maintained, and she could make out some horses grazing in the distance. Farther off she could hear the growl of a tractor's engine on the grass-scented June breeze. She'd have found this place relaxing if she weren't so wound up.

"Avery, you said?" He released her hand, and she waited for some sort of recognition to dawn. It didn't.

"Avery Southerly."

He raised his eyebrows—still no recognition. She'd

come out to Montana to introduce herself to her father, and she'd known it would be difficult. Since her mother passed away, she had a new desire to meet the father she'd never known. However, she was nervous enough that she'd come with an excuse: an advertisement for a cook at the Harmon Ranch that she'd spotted on a bulletin board in the coffee shop. If she couldn't suss up the courage to tell him everything right away, then she'd simply apply for the job and wait for the right moment...maybe even get to know her father a little bit before there was all the pressure of surprise paternity.

He nodded toward the flyer in her hand. "I assume you're here for the cook position."

She looked down. It was now or never...

"Yes." She gave a decisive nod. "I'm applying for the job, sir."

"Glad you are because the competition is very thin right about now." He laughed.

Well, that took care of that. Louis nodded toward the house and started walking away, so she followed him.

"The team isn't too fussy," he said over his shoulder. "They like the basics—griddle cakes, bacon, eggs, baked beans, steak once a week and as much corn bread as you can bake."

He led the way along a path toward the side door of the low ranch-style house. It was large and sprawling, with one wing dedicated to a three-door garage. He pulled open the screen door and gestured her through.

"You *can* make corn bread, can't you?" he asked.

"Uh—yes. I can make corn bread."

She'd made corn bread once, at least, from a recipe

she found online. She wasn't a great cook, to be honest… She wasn't completely inept in a kitchen, but she knew her limitations, and this idea was starting to unravel in her mind already. She should just come out with it—tell him the truth—but *Actually, I'm here to inform you that I'm your daughter* just wouldn't come out of her mouth.

The kitchen table was stacked with books and ledgers, along with a smattering of papers. A horse bridle hung on the back of a kitchen chair, and Louis took off his hat and tossed it on the seat. He ran his hand over his salt-and-pepper gray hair. He definitely looked like he could be somebody's dad, but *hers*?

At the age of twenty-four, Avery wasn't looking for a father figure, just some answers. She wanted to know about the man who sired her and the story of his connection to her mother—the story her mother refused to tell. Maybe she could gather up some medical history. But she didn't have a lot of time for this visit. Back in Salina, Kansas, she was about to reopen her mother's flower shop, which had been closed since her mother entered hospice. She had two weeks until the June 24 opening date, and she wanted to make the most of that time. That store was her home—the place where she'd spent her formative years. But first, she wanted to learn about her father, whom her mom had only confessed on her deathbed.

"Coffee?"

"No, thanks."

"You aren't from Hope, are you?" he asked. "I'd recognize you if you were."

"No, I'm from Kansas," she replied.

"But you're not in Kansas anymore," Louis quipped, then chortled to himself at his little joke. "Sorry, that was a dumb one. You probably hear that all the time, don't you?"

Avery smiled. "Only when I leave the state."

She'd imagined what her father would be like a thousand times since she was a little girl, trying to piece together what he might look like from her own reflection in the mirror. Did he have red hair like hers? Did he hate tomatoes, too? But never in all her imaginings had she come up with a man who looked like Louis.

"Well, I'll level with you, Avery," Louis said. "I need a cook to start tomorrow, and you are the one and only applicant. I'm not too picky. If you can cook, and if you have a clean criminal record, I'll give you a try."

"Thanks for the opportunity, sir," she said with a smile. "If you can show me the ropes…"

She was afraid to tell him the truth because he might not be thrilled to find out he had an illegitimate daughter, and from what she knew, her father had never been told about her existence. But she was wary for herself, too. She'd wanted a father so badly for so long, but only recently had she considered the possibility that her biological father might not be worthy of *her*. Her mother had given her an identity—they were the Southerlys. But who was she now that her mother was gone? And did Louis Harmon fit into that?

"The ropes" might not be enough to let her pass muster, but maybe she could search a few recipes online and not look like a complete incompetent. YouTube tutorials could prove useful…until she was certain that she wanted to declare herself.

"I pay the going rate." He scratched a number on a slip of paper and handed it over.

"That seems fair." Actually, she had no idea what the going rate was for ranch cooks, but she felt the need to commit to the part now that she'd started. This was ridiculous! She didn't need extra money, and she didn't need a job. But Louis seemed so pleased to have a cook that she just couldn't let him down. Yet. She'd have to eventually.

The side door opened and a cowboy stepped inside, taking his hat off as the screen door slammed behind him. He was a tall man with sandy blond hair and a slim build. His bare forearms were roped with muscle and darkened by a tan. His face was lined from the sun, and blue eyes moved over her in quick evaluation, pausing just a beat longer than necessary.

"Ah, Hank." Louis nodded to the newcomer. "Perfect timing. We have a cook."

"Great." Hank glanced toward her again, this time with more curiosity. He looked to be in his midthirties, and there was something in his perfectly professional gaze that sped her heart up just a little. Maybe it was the laser focus he directed at her, appraising her on the spot. Avery gave him a nod.

"Hank Granger is my ranch manager," Louis said. "You'll be answering to him. He can show you the canteen and make sure you're set up."

Hank leaned over and shook her hand, his grasp firm but gentle.

"Welcome aboard," he said, a slight smile quirking up one side of his mouth. "And you are—"

"Avery Southerly," she replied, pulling her hand back. She glanced toward Louis to see if repeating her name had sparked anything in his memory, but the older man's expression didn't change.

"I'll get you settled," Hank said. "We need you to stay on-site for this position, the hours being what they are. I hope that isn't a problem for you." When she shrugged her compliance, he added, "There's a room in the bunkhouse—a private one—for the cook, so you should be comfortable enough. But first we'll need some ID so we can do a background check."

"Of course." Avery provided the necessary identification, and Louis disappeared into the next room where the rattle and moan of an old photocopier filtered through the open door. When Louis came back into the kitchen, he handed back her ID and had her sign the bottom of an employment form. This was getting official quickly.

"I might as well show you around," Hank said. "Mr. Harmon can give us a call if there's any problem. Is there anything else, boss?"

"No, that should cover it," Louis replied. "It's nice to meet you, Avery. Hank will take good care of you, but I'll stop by later on this evening to see if you need anything."

"Thanks," she said, her insides roiling with misgiving. Was she really going to cook for this ranch for the next two weeks? But the other option was to announce who she was now and probably be shown the door for having misled them this far. Or she could take a few days to get to know Louis a little bit, and then say something. Hopefully, after a little time getting to know her, he'd understand why she did this.

Hank led the way, pushing open the screen door to let her pass ahead of him. She was struck by how tall he was as she stepped past him—she only came up to his shoulder—and how he smelled of musk, hay and sunshine. He stood motionless until she was past, then followed, releasing the door behind him.

A warm breeze pushed Avery's hair away from her face, and the screen door closed with a bang. She had just officially met her father.

HANK GRANGER LED the way around the house to where his old blue Chevy pickup waited. He glanced over at the sad-eyed new hire. She was pretty—more than pretty, if he were honest. She had golden red hair that spilled down her shoulders and skin the color of new milk. Her eyes were flecked with green, and she had freckles across her nose and on the tops of her shoulders, not covered by her white tank top. And those jeans fit rather well...

Blast it, he wasn't supposed to be checking her out, and he shouldn't be noticing that scoop of her collarbone, either. Mr. Harmon relied on Hank for his professionalism, and dalliances with other employees were strictly forbidden on this ranch. This was more than a job for Hank. This was home, and he had no intention of messing up a good thing. Besides, she was *young.* Way under thirty—she was too inexperienced to be weighed down with a pessimistic SOB like him. That should be enough to keep his mind on the straight and narrow.

There had been something in the way she was looking at Louis back there—cautiously, expectantly. She'd wanted something from him, and not just the job. There was more to her arrival than a simple desire for employment. Maybe she was the gold-digging type, and she'd sniffed out a wealthy widower. Whatever it was, this Avery had ulterior motives—he was willing to bet on it.

"So where are you from?" Hank asked as they reached the truck. He pulled open the passenger-side door and gestured her inside.

"Salina, Kansas," she replied, hopping up into the seat.

A pretty out-of-towner looking for ranch work. She was no cowgirl. She wore slim Nike runners, and her nails looked too good. He came around the driver's side.

"So what brings you to Hope?" he asked as he slid into the driver's seat and slammed the door.

She paused a breath longer than necessary, then said, "My mom grew up in Hope, and I wanted to see it."

"Alone?" he prodded.

"She passed away in April."

Ouch. Hank shot her an apologetic look. "Sorry about that."

She smiled in reply, but it didn't reach her eyes. Hank pulled away from the house. The wheels of his truck crunched over the gravel and onto the drive that led away from the barn and toward the bunkhouse and canteen for the workers. Warm afternoon sunlight bathed the land. Bees circled over wildflowers in the ditches, and Hank slapped a mosquito on his arm. It was the season for them. He drove past the nearest pasture, and the cows looked up, chewing in slow, grinding circles, their liquid eyes following the truck as it passed them.

"So what was your mom's name?" he asked. He was curious—if her family was from Hope, maybe he could place her.

"Winona Southerly."

It didn't ring any bells, but if Avery had never seen Hope, then her mother must have left town a good—he glanced at Avery from the corner of his eye—twenty-five years ago, in a rough estimation. He wouldn't have known her mother—he'd have been ten at the time.

"You have any other family around here?" he asked.

"No, my mom was living with an elderly aunt who passed away when I was a kid," she said. "But I wanted to see Hope. Mom used to tell me some stories about rope swings and swimming in a canal, back in the seventies when kids could roam feral."

He smiled at the mental picture. Yeah, those were the days. He'd been a kid in the eighties, and he'd still been pretty feral. The town of Hope was small enough that people trusted each other—maybe more than they should.

"So you wanted to see it," he concluded.

"With her gone, I just—" She pulled her hair away from her face. "I guess it makes it feel like she's not completely gone."

"Yeah, I get it."

He knew a fair bit about loss, about dealing with that empty hole in your chest. He'd gotten divorced five years back, and that had been a gut-wrenching loss. Vickie had started up with some guy online. Hank used to be a whole lot more trusting. *He's just a friend* turned into *He understands me and you don't even try,* which eventually turned into her packing her bags and leaving. Vickie had been wrong—he *had* tried. He'd tried really hard to understand what she needed, what she wanted. He hadn't been some passive guy letting his woman walk off—he'd done everything he knew how. It just hadn't been enough.

"Do your parents live around here?" Avery asked.

He pulled himself back to the present. "No, they're in Florida."

"Hmm." She smiled. "That's nice."

His parents loved Skype—always calling at inopportune times, crowding in front of their tablet so they could both beam at him from their motor home. They were so proud of that thing—they still gave him virtual tours. *You wouldn't believe how spacious it is, Hank! Look at the depth of these cupboards... Can you see it? Hold on, I'll put on a light... Can you see it now?*

Hank was approaching the barracks now—a long, low building on the crest of a hill, overlooking the pasture and a winding creek that watered it.

"Okay," he said pulling himself away from personal topics. "I guess I should tell you the job requirements. First of all, Mr. Harmon has a rule against employees becoming romantically involved. There is no wiggle room there. If you're caught, you'll be fired. No second chances."

She nodded. "Okay. Fair enough."

"I really can't stress it enough." He eyed her, waiting for some sort of response, but she just met his gaze with mild curiosity. That was the biggest rule out of the way. "You'll be providing breakfast, lunch, dinner and snacks for thirty-five employees. Breakfast is at 6:00 a.m. sharp, lunches are packed and supper is at five. You can't be late—our scheduling relies on prompt meals."

She didn't say anything, but when he glanced over, she was chewing the side of her cheek. Nerves? So the cooking—that's where he got a reaction from her?

"You think you can handle that?" he asked.

"Sure." She shot him a smile that was just an eyelash shy of being convincing.

"We're looking at high-protein meals, and don't skimp on the carbs. The guys can eat a lot—they burn it off out there, so they have to be able to fill up. Obviously, we need balanced meals, but you've got to be able to cook according to a budget…"

As he talked, he could feel tension emanating from her through the cab, and when he pulled to a stop in front of the barracks, he eyed her curiously.

"You want to see your room first, or the kitchen?" he asked.

"Uh…" She looked out the window. "The kitchen, I suppose."

They got out of the truck and he led the way toward the canteen. Their last cook had given notice, but Louis hadn't been able to fill the position in time to fill the gap. This was the first day without a regular cook on premises, and the stock of muffins and sandwiches had been worked through pretty fast. He pushed open the door, leading the way past the tables and toward the kitchen in the back.

When they emerged into the quiet, cool room, the look on Avery's face was pure panic.

"Exactly how much experience do you have?" Hank asked skeptically.

She heaved a sigh and shook her head. "Zero."

What? He stared at her, aghast. She had absolutely no experience, and she'd applied for this job? What had she been thinking? And why had Louis hired her so quickly? He supposed they didn't have many options—they needed someone, and one of the ranch hands would be just as bad as an inexperienced stranger. At least the ranch hand would be able to do his job out in the field if they had this woman in the kitchen.

"Let me get this straight…" he said slowly.

"Should I leave?" she interrupted, turning to look him in the face for the first time. Her green eyes glittered, and she crossed her arms across her chest—protective or defiant, he wasn't sure which.

"Can you at least cook?" he asked. That would be something. Cooking in large batches could be learned… couldn't it? If she could at least make some batches of oatmeal, muffins, fry up some burgers…

Avery visibly winced.

"Are you saying you can't cook at all?" he demanded.

"I'm capable of cooking," she retorted. "I'm twenty-four and I've fed myself for some time now." She sighed. "I've just never been…good at it."

He closed his eyes and suppressed a moan.

"I'll go." She moved toward the door. "I'm sorry to have wasted your time."

It wasn't how pretty she was, or those glittering green eyes. It certainly wasn't the smattering of freckles that drew his gaze as she turned away…it was the knowledge that without her here, a valuable ranch hand would be taken away from his work and set to manning the kitchen until they could find someone else, and after three weeks of advertising, she was the only one to show up.

"Wait," he said gruffly. "You're already hired. Let's give you a try."

"Are you sure?" she asked. "Because you don't need to do this. If someone else is a better fit—"

"There isn't anyone else," he said. "If you're willing to learn, I guess I'll teach you what I know, and we'll get these guys fed."

She pulled out her cell phone. "YouTube tutorials might help."

So that was where they were at. This was going to be a long day, he could tell, but a suspicion nagged at the back of his mind. He might need to keep her on for now, but he also meant to keep an eye on her. After Hank's divorce, the Harmon family had been really good to him, and he felt like he owed Louis more than just to follow his job requirements. And Avery gave off the vibe, back in the house, of a woman with an ulterior motive.

Now he discovered that she'd applied for a position she had zero experience for, and she was offering to walk away far too quickly for someone who needed the job despite her inexperience. His hackles were up.

He didn't know the real reason Avery had shown up, but he'd figure it out. He didn't like secrets; he was the kind of man who wanted things transparent, out in the open. Secrets always hurt someone, he'd found. Hank knew firsthand what kind man Louis Harmon was. As ranch manager, it was his job to know what was going on, and he took that job very seriously.

"Alright," Hank said. "Let me show you where you'll be staying, then I should probably start showing you what I can in the kitchen. We need to whip up dinner for the hands. That is, if you're ready to start early—"

"Sure," she said. "I'll be happy to."

That was a relief, because right now, he didn't have much choice.

Chapter Two

Hank led the way to Avery's room, located at the far end of the bunkhouse. The building was empty, their footsteps echoing, and Avery could only assume that was because the other employees were working at this hour. The hallways smelled male—like socks and stale cigarettes.

Avery stood back as Hank unlocked a door at the end of the hallway and swung it open. He held out the key, and when she took it, her fingers brushed over his calloused fingertips. There wasn't much room in the doorway, and as she moved past him, she could feel his body heat.

"This is where you'll sleep," he said. "You have your own bathroom through there."

Avery glanced around. There was a bed topped with a patchwork quilt, an outdated dresser, a wobbly wardrobe and a small but private bathroom with a tub large enough to actually take a bath. Thanks to a cracked-open window, her room smelled fresh and clean. When she peeked outside, she had a magnificent view of pasture and the main barn. That was something. And if she counted the blessing that she wouldn't have to share facilities like the ranch hands did, she couldn't complain. Even settling in wouldn't be difficult. Her suitcase was in the trunk of her car, so that would be easy enough. But as she stood in the center of the room, a giggle bubbled up inside her.

If her mother were still living, she'd find this hilarious, too. Well, maybe not the fact that Avery was in Hope, looking for details about her mother's past… Winona wouldn't have liked that at all. But the outrageousness of being hired as a ranch cook—that would have tickled her funny bone. Winona used to tell her, *Men expect a pretty girl to be able to cook. And you're pretty, sweetheart. So you'd better learn how to cook, or learn how to let 'em down easy.* Avery hadn't learned.

Winona Southerly was a strong woman with her own idea of how things should be. She raised Avery to go to church every week, rain or shine. Winona's Wilderness, the flower shop her mother opened when Avery was in the second grade, had been closed Sunday mornings, opening at 2:00 p.m. No exceptions. She'd been strict that way. When Avery complained that she didn't want to go to Sunday school, her mother would retort, *So the store is closed for nothing then? I'm losing business as we speak. We're going to church. You could use a few positive influences, my girl.* And heaven help them if they were late. But she'd had a sense of humor, too. Every time she lost something—a pair of scissors, an umbrella—she declared it had been raptured and *the Lord needed it more than I did, I suppose.* Church people never knew exactly how seriously to take her on that—whether she needed a theological tune-up, or if they should just laugh along. She liked pushing the envelope, keeping people guessing. Those were the memories that made Avery's heart ache with loneliness. Life wasn't going to be the same without Mom.

"Will it do?" Hank asked behind her.

Avery turned and nodded. "It'll be just fine."

He nodded, then his direct blue gaze met hers and she felt heat rise in her cheeks. This ranch manager was just so…male. She kept noticing things like the stubble on his jawline, or the latent strength in those large hands of his. She couldn't do anything about it, though. She was here for a reason, and this cowboy didn't factor into that.

"So what is Mr. Harmon like?" she asked.

Hank shrugged. "A decent guy. He doesn't cut corners. He pays on time."

That wasn't exactly what she was looking for, but then, she was only supposed to be an employee.

"Does he have a family?" she asked. "Here at the ranch, I mean."

"He's a widower, but he has two kids, Olivia and Owen. They're twins. You'll see them around."

He had kids… That meant she had siblings. The thought was surprising and pleasing. She'd wanted a brother or sister growing up, but that hadn't happened. So siblings—someone else in the world she shared genes with—she liked that. And twins ran in the family… That might be good to know for future reference.

"How old are they?" she asked.

"They're in…" Hank paused. "I want to say tenth grade. Maybe eleventh? High school students, though."

She had a brother and a sister…and a father. While the thought of having more family was pleasing, it was also more intimidating. Those kids might not find her existence quite as comforting as she found theirs, especially at their age. They'd be territorial, and understandably.

"What happened to their mom?" she asked.

"She passed away a couple of years ago," he said. "Riding accident. Some workers hadn't locked a gate. The wind pushed it open, the horse spooked and she fell. Quick as that."

"That's too bad." She wondered what Louis's wife had been like. Perhaps a little bit like her mother in some way? She'd come to the conclusion that Louis's relationship with her mother hadn't been long or meaningful, or Louis would have shown some sort of reaction at her last name, if nothing else. She'd been sure her last name would spark some memories about her mother, but nothing? Had Winona been that forgettable for him?

Hank led the way back out of the room. Avery locked the door behind them and followed him down the long hall and out into the sunlight. She paused, looking around. The main house was visible on the crest of a hill a couple of miles off, and the horses shone bronze as they grazed in the field next to it. From their vantage point, slightly higher than the rest of the ranch, she could make out a wider view of the patchwork effect of adjacent fields. Early afternoon sunlight splashed over the distant barn that was visible from her bedroom window, and a tractor towing a trailer filled with hay crept along a gravel road, clouds of dust billowing up behind it. The canteen, which hunched next to the bunkhouse, was a low wooden building with a hitching post out front.

Hank didn't seem like he'd say much else, and she wondered if she'd overdone it. But her time here was limited, and if she were going to take this job in order to find out a little more about her father, then she'd have to ask questions.

"How long have you worked here?" she asked, changing tack.

"Twelve years," he replied, then turned toward her just before they reached the door to the canteen. "Long enough to know the boss really well. He's been good to me, and I'm not about to gossip about his personal business. I've told you all I'm going to tell you."

Heat suffused Avery's cheeks. "Didn't mean to offend."

"If you want to talk, let's talk about you," Hank said, pulling open the door and letting her go inside first. The canteen was cool and dark, and it took a moment for Avery's eyes to adjust.

"This way." Hank moved past her. She stood there for a moment, glad for the darkness that could hide the color she knew was in her face. She didn't like being chastised. Maybe this cowboy thought of her as some youngster compared to him, but she was far from naive, and far from being meek. Avery moved forward and her shin connected with something solid she couldn't make out in the dim light.

"Ouch!" She closed her eyes in a grimace, and then opened them to find she could see a little better now.

It had been a bench in her way, and Hank now stood in front of her. He was a big man, but his presence was even larger than his physical size. He always seemed to be inspecting her when he looked at her like that, and she found it irritating.

"You okay?" His voice was rough but gentle, and in the dim light his closeness made her feel slightly flustered. He obviously didn't trust her, but he wasn't being a complete jerk, either.

"Fine," she said. "I can see better now."

"That's good." He walked away from her again, and she followed in his wake, moving around tables and chairs toward the swinging kitchen door ahead. He flicked the switch as they went inside, and the room buzzed with florescent light.

"So how long are you here for?" Hank asked. He opened a drawer and tossed her a white apron.

"It won't be long-term. I just needed a job while passing through," she said cautiously. Obviously, they'd need to plan for the future around here, and she felt a pang of guilt. "Look, truthfully, I need to be back in Salina by June twenty-fourth. So I'll be here for a couple of weeks. You'll definitely want to keep looking for a cook."

"Ah." He paused, eyed her for a moment. "Thanks for letting me know."

She shrugged, but felt like a fraud—could he sense that?

"You have someone waiting for you back in Salina?" he asked.

She eyed the kitchen appliances—two stoves, a large industrial fridge, a massive mixer on one counter.

"Someone?" She smiled wryly. "No. But I'm reopening my mom's flower shop when I get back. I was pretty much raised in that shop. I went there every day after school and did my homework at the front counter."

That store was more of a home than their little apartment had been, and when her mother died, it was the only stability she had left.

"So you're a florist," he said, shooting her an odd look.

"My mom was a florist," Avery corrected him. "I worked at the bank, but when mom passed away and her life insurance came through, I quit so I could concentrate on her business."

In college, she'd changed her major so many times that when she finally did graduate, it was with a generic arts degree. She'd never quite known what she wanted do with herself, what she wanted to be, and she realized after her mother had passed away that she'd relied on Winona for her identity. She was her mother's daughter—but now?

"Don't like counting other people's money?" he asked with a small smile.

"It was just a job." She shrugged. "But my mom's store is home in a lot of ways, and having it just empty out and shut down…" She sighed. "It was too heartbreaking."

"So what are you doing here?" he pressed.

She eyed him for a moment. She wondered if he were a distrustful man in general, or if he was just concerned about the stability of his staff. Possibly a bit of both, but she found herself mildly intrigued by him, too. He was older than she was—old enough that she'd call him sir if she trampled his foot in the street—but she was also very aware of him, of his movement, of the way he looked at her. She ran her hand over a countertop.

"I'm trying to learn about my mom," she said. "She didn't say much about her childhood, and now that she's gone, I want to figure out that side of her that she kept hidden."

"Would she want you to?"

His question was unexpected, and she felt a twang of annoyance. What did he know about her relationship with her mother, or what Winona would have wanted?

"Probably not," she admitted, tears misting her eyes. "But she's gone, so…"

Dying had been the worst thing her mother had ever done, because Avery still needed her. She might be a grown woman, but she wasn't finished being mothered yet. Her mom had never wanted her to meet her dad, or to even know his name, but since she'd gone and heartlessly died, Avery would have to make these choices on her own. Wherever Winona was—raptured with the scissors?—Avery hoped her mother could forgive her, because she had come to town in search of the very answers Winona had kept hidden all these years. And perhaps while she learned who her mother used to be, she could figure out who she was without her mother in her life.

Hank opened the fridge and pulled out three large, cellophane-wrapped packages of cubed steak and tossed them onto the stainless steel center table with a bang.

"The last cook suggested beef stew."

Avery glanced around the kitchen, taking in the large

pots, the hanging spatulas, the knives in neat rows held along magnetic strips on the wall. Beef stew. It sounded simple enough. Beef, carrots, potatoes, broth. Onions— couldn't forget those. Yes, this was under control.

Hank's cell phone rang, and he picked up the call. "Yeah?…Okay…No, that's a priority…Okay, I'll meet you there." He hung up the phone.

"Is there a problem?" she asked.

"A water pipe leak affecting the water pressure for some sprinklers. I've got to look into it." He paused. "So will you be okay here?"

"I can do this," she said, her confidence returning.

"Yeah?" He looked a little wary, but she was armed with YouTube and a massive pot. What could possibly go wrong?

"You're cooking for thirty-five," he said, nodding toward the stove. "That pot should be full."

"Dinner's at five?" she asked.

"Five sharp." He turned toward the door, and she pulled out her phone. She knew she'd find online videos and recipes and cooking tips galore. Stew was within the realm of possibility. Hank paused at the door and pulled out a little pad of paper, scratched a number on it and placed it on the center table. "Call me if you get into trouble."

Nice to say, but she highly doubted that kitchen woes would trump anything else he had going in the rest of the ranch. She'd sort things out on her own.

THAT DAY THE work in the field took longer than Hank anticipated. The water pressure was down to a dribble out there, and the fix was more complicated than they'd originally thought. He and the men didn't ride back to the canteen until ten past five, and they'd have to head back out after they ate for another go at it. Hank was both hungry and nervous. There were thirty-five hungry workers needing a decent meal, and he'd left a woman they didn't know in charge of the kitchen, hoping for the best.

Hank bounced along the gravel road that meandered back up toward the barracks and the canteen. The radio was on low, a country song filling up the space between the roar of the engine and the rattle of equipment in the back. He'd been thinking about Avery the entire time he was searching for that blasted leak, telling himself repeatedly he was just worried about the food. But it was less noble than that. He'd never thought of himself as a guy with a type, but if he had one, she was it. Slender, cute, fair. Maybe it was just the fact that there weren't a lot of other women around here.

Hank parked his truck in front of the building, hopped out and slammed the door with a satisfying bang. The canteen had two large, old-fashioned wagon wheels on either side of the double doors, which were already propped open. Some of the men had arrived ahead of him, their truck already parked in a spot in front. His stomach rumbled. Beef stew would hit the spot tonight. It had been a long day, but the job wasn't yet done, and he needed a solid meal.

As Hank stepped inside, he was met with the murmur of voices, some laughter, the clink of cutlery—all normal. The smell, though… It wasn't just the press of sweaty bodies, it was something else he couldn't quite identify...

"Hey, Hank." Bernie, one of the ranch hands sat in front of a bowl of stew, two dinner rolls next to it. "Have you seen the new cook?"

"Yeah, I showed her around," Hank replied.

"Well, thank you for hiring that one," he said with a grin. "She's hot."

There was a chorus of laughter and a few crude comments. Hank shot them a flat stare. Hot or not—and he wasn't arguing how good-looking she was—she wasn't here to be ogled. She was here to cook. There were workplace rules about sexual harassment and about fraternizing with the staff, rules he was following, too. When Louis's wife, Carla, had died in that riding accident, it had been because a couple of workers were literally having a roll in the hay. Her death was preventable, and while those workers had been fired, Louis set up an ironclad rule about workplace dalliances.

"How's the food?" Hank asked. He leaned closer to the bowl and discovered the source of the "off" smell. "Oh, man..."

"It's—" Bernie shrugged. "It's served by the pretty redhead. I'll have seconds."

The man across the table from them, Ivan, was chewing a piece of beef, his jaw moving in slow rotations. Hank paused and watched him chew for another ten seconds.

"You gonna swallow that?" Hank asked.

Ivan slowly shook his head. "It's like leather," he said past the meat in his mouth. "I can't get it down."

There didn't seem to be any open complaining, in-terestingly enough. Had a man served that meal, there'd have been a riot. Avery stood across the room, bending down to offer more bread to one of the ranch hands, whose eyes were fixed on her cleavage. Her red hair tumbled down in front of her shoulders—no hairnet, apparently—and her smile was bright. This was a rough bunch of guys, and Avery probably had no idea what she was getting herself into here. He headed toward her, and when Avery saw him, she shot him a smile.

"Hi," he said, clapping a hand onto the shoulder of the ranch hand who had been ogling Avery's chest. The man dropped his gaze to his bowl immediately.

"Served on time," she said, looking quite satisfied with herself. "And everyone seems to love it."

"Mmm. Delicious," the ranch hand said on cue, and Hank suppressed the urge to roll his eyes. Yeah, they all seemed to be willing to compliment the meal, if only to get a little of the cook's personal attention. And for that, Hank couldn't blame them entirely. There wasn't a whole lot of female contact out here, and they had to wait until they went into Hope on their days off for a beer at the Honky Tonk in order to get a woman to look at them straight. He'd have to have a word with Avery in private.

"You must be starving," Avery said. "Let me get you a bowl."

"Sure," he said. "In the kitchen."

She shot him a quizzical look, but complied and they headed through the swinging door into relative privacy. The kitchen was hot from cooking, and the pot was still on the stove. She stepped onto a stool next to the stove so she could reach inside and she scooped him up a big bowl of stew. He grabbed a bun and took a bite of the crusty roll, holding the proffered bowl of stew in the other hand for the time being.

"You, too," he said, nodding to the pot. "I couldn't possibly try this before you do."

Avery bent back over the pot to fill her own bowl, and he watched her move. She was feminine—an odd thing to notice about a woman. Weren't all women feminine? But there was something soft and lithe about her, something that should smell like flowers—even though he couldn't smell anything but that stew right now.

"It wasn't so bad," Avery said, picking up a spoon from the counter. "I was a little worried at first—" She dipped the spoon into the bowl and blew on it a couple of times before she took a bite. Her expression changed as she pulled the spoon from her mouth, and she chewed slowly.

"Well?" he asked.

"It's, um…" She swallowed. "I think something went wrong."

"Yeah?" he asked. "What did you do to it?"

"I followed the directions!" She shot him an annoyed look. "To the T, might I add. Beef stew. I have no idea what went wrong. Except there wasn't any red wine."

"Yeah, we don't tend to cook with red wine out here," he said wryly.

"I may have replaced the red wine with red wine vinegar."

He grimaced. Vinegar in beef stew? What had she

been thinking? But she looked so let down. Avery ran her hand through her hair, tugging those loose waves away from her face. It was the disappointment in those green-flecked eyes. She'd actually thought she'd done well, and the other guys had let her believe it. He normally wouldn't make much effort for a cook's feelings...

"Pass me some salt," he said with a sigh.

"You're going to eat it?" she asked. "I'm sure I can rummage up something else for you."

"It's what's for dinner," he replied. "I'll eat what my men are eating."

And he wasn't pleased about that. He was hungry— as were all the guys out there. They'd worked a long day, and they needed a decent meal at the end of that. He was grumpy, he was hungry and the glop in his bowl was possibly the worst stew he'd eaten in his life. And that included cattle drives where the one who drew the shortest straw had to cook.

"Breakfast will be better," she said. "Eggs, bacon, corn bread...that's hard to ruin."

He'd thought the same thing about the stew.

"Tell you what," he said. "I'll meet you here at 4:00 a.m., and we'll work on it together. We'll have to make the pack lunches, too. At least that way, if the guys don't like the grub, they can blame me, too."

And at the very least, they'd get an edible lunch.

"But *they* seem to like it..." She looked toward the swinging door, her pale brows knitted. Had she really not figured out how gorgeous she was and what that did to the common male?

"Yeah..." He shot her a wry look. "They seem to."

She wasn't going to be sticking around Hope for long, but while she was here, maybe they could manage to get some decent grub.

Chapter Three

The evening shadows stretched out long and deep, and Avery stood by a fence, her foot on a rail as she watched the sun sink steadily lower. The sky was turning a misty pink, crimson bleeding out along the horizon. The fields glowed gold in the sunset, cattle dotting the lush greenery. A couple of roads snaked across the land, empty and lonesome.

Should I even be here?

Today had been strange in every way. When she arrived in Hope, she hadn't known what to expect. Her mother had always been secretive about who her father was, and when she confessed a name on her deathbed, that's where she'd stopped. Louis Harmon. No more details. By Louis's reaction to hearing her name, Avery was assuming that Winona had never told Louis about the daughter they'd made together. Why not? What could she have possibly gained by hiding Avery from him? Louis seemed kind. He was obviously respected by his employees. Hank sure seemed to think a lot of him.

It didn't make sense, but at least Winona had given Avery his name before she died. That name linked her to a family she'd never known about—a family that very well might not want to know about her. It was strange to think about herself as orphaned at twenty-four, but that was how she felt. She'd counted on her mother for more than she realized—for her gut reaction to the guys Avery dated, for her optimistic view of the future, for her skill in running the flower shop. Mom knew how to make the perfect arrangement for that finicky bride. She knew how to comfort the bereaved family buying flowers for a funeral. She always managed to look right through whichever guy Avery was dating and figure him out before Avery even managed to. *Sweetheart, he's not as committed as you are. If he's saying good-night by nine, I'm willing to bet he's got another date lined up for ten.*

It had always been her and Mom against the world, and now it was suddenly just her. And while Avery was perfectly able to run her life, the hole her mother left behind was still raw.

A truck's engine rumbled behind her, and she turned to see Louis pull up in front of the bunkhouse. The truck was new—glossy black with shining chrome. You could tell who the boss was around here. The older man hopped out of the truck and slammed the door. He spotted her by the fence and waved.

Avery headed toward him and shot him a smile.

"Evening," he said.

"Hi," she replied. "Nice night."

"Sure is." He shook her hand with that same crushing grip from earlier. "Are you settled in okay?"

"Yes, I'm fine, thanks." She crossed her arms. "Served my first meal."

"I heard." Something flickered across his expression. He must have heard how bad it tasted, too. So was this it? Was he going to fire her? She almost wished he would, then she'd be forced to tell him why she'd really come and get it over with.

"I know it wasn't the best stew," she began.

"I'm not worried about it. Hank assures me that it's under control. He's your boss, so he's the one you need to impress."

Great. She hadn't done a great job in impressing him so far.

"Alright. Well…thank you for being patient with me."

"Hank also mentioned you've got about two weeks here. We appreciate the honesty on that. It's still good to have you here to fill the vacancy while we keep looking for a permanent cook."

"I'm glad it will work for both of us," she said. And she was. She hadn't wanted to mislead them. "I should have mentioned it to you earlier. It all got away from me."

Louis was silent for a moment, and he looked out toward the fields and the sunset. His weathered face softened.

"I knew a Winona Southerly a long time ago. Any relation?" he asked.

"My mother," she said, and her voice trembled slightly as the words came out.

"Really?" Louis's eyebrows shot up and he looked at her in surprise. "You're Winona Southerly's daughter?"

"Yes." Avery smiled. "I've been told I look like her—if I were blond."

"Hmm." He nodded. "Yes, I can see it—I should have noticed before. Where is your mother now?"

"She passed away," Avery replied. "Breast cancer."

"Oh…" Louis's expression fell and he shook his head. "I'm sorry. She was quite the gal. I knew her… well, a long time ago. What did she end up doing with her life?"

"She had me young," Avery said. "She worked odd jobs for a few years and inherited some money when my grandmother passed away. She used it to open a flower shop in Salina."

"Hmm." He nodded slowly. "Sounds like a good life."

"Too short, though," Avery said. "She was forty-three. I'm actually here trying to find out a little bit more about her…and her relationships."

An awkward look crossed Louis's face. He was silent for a moment, then said, "She was a good person—fun, sympathetic. She was a good friend."

Friend. Right. Obviously, she'd been a little more than that.

"So you knew her well?" Avery pressed.

"We were kids," he said with a shake of his head. "When I knew your mother she wanted to marry a senator, learn some bull riding—" he smiled sadly "—and open a flower shop."

Avery hadn't realized that a flower shop had been

part of her mother's dreams back then. She knew her mother had opened the business so that she could be her own boss and be there for Avery after school. But she hadn't realized that shop had been a dream fulfilled. The bull riding didn't seem to fit, though.

"Did she get married?" Louis asked.

"Once," Avery replied. "It lasted three years, and after the divorce she focused on me." That made it sound like she didn't have any other options, somehow, so she added, "There were a couple of other gentlemen from church who used to come by the shop and chat with her, though. If she'd not gotten sick, she might have married again."

"Church?" Louis took off his hat and slapped it against his thigh. "And you came to find out about your mother's time in Hope, did you?"

He'd been talking to Hank, it seemed.

"Yes," she said.

He chewed the side of his cheek and nodded several times.

"You knew her…" she prodded.

"Yeah, I did," he agreed. "If you're wanting to find out more about her, Winona went to the local high school. You might find some old photos there. And people knew her…lots of people knew her."

"What church did she go to?" Avery asked. That might be another avenue to sleuth out, and perhaps thinking about Winona would spark some old memories for Louis.

Louis chuckled. "She wasn't much into church when she lived here, I'm afraid."

That was a surprise, because Winona had been a spiritual woman as far back as Avery could remember.

"I guess we all change over the years," Louis said slowly. "We grow and learn, and let go of a few mistakes."

His words sank down into the pit of her stomach. Was he referring to Winona, or to himself? Was that what Winona was to him—a mistake? Somehow, Avery hadn't considered that option, but obviously Louis had married someone else and started a family of his own. Maybe that was the way he remembered Winona, after all. A wave of resentment crashed over her... Her mother deserved better than that, a whole lot better. Unless Louis was lying. Maybe he didn't want his balance here upset.

"Did my mother ever contact you?" she asked a little more curtly than intended.

"No." Louis frowned slightly, her intention seeming to miss him. "She didn't have any reason, that I know of."

"I just—" Avery shook her head. This wasn't the right moment to announce it all. "I was curious about why she would walk away from this town and never mention it again until her last days."

That was a roundabout way of getting at it. Why had her mother walked away from here, from Louis, and never looked back?

"She didn't talk about Hope?" Louis asked.

"Nothing more than to say she'd grown up here," Avery replied. "And that she never wanted to come back."

"Oh." Louis sucked in a breath, then blew out a sigh. "She must have had her reasons…I suppose."

"You don't know why?" Avery pressed.

Louis was silent for a moment, and then he fixed his dark gaze on Avery and said quietly, "You say she was a church lady in Kansas. Right?"

"Yes, she was very devout," Avery replied.

"Well, she wasn't like that here, you see," he said quietly. "She was—" He pressed his lips together into a thin line. "She was a fun girl, and she knew how to let loose. She…knew how to have a good time, and broke a few hearts. You get my drift?"

Was he suggesting what she thought he was? Anger boiled up inside her. Her mother had only been gone for a couple of months, and to hear her spoken of like that…

"Are you saying she slept around?" Avery snapped. "Because I don't believe that for a second! If you knew her like you claim—"

"Look, I'm only saying this because you'll find out anyway if you start asking around," Louis said, apology written all over his face. "But your mom looked for love in all the wrong places, and it sounds like she started looking in the right places when she got to Kansas. So you've got to give her credit for that."

The tone was gentle, almost too gentle, but his words sank in. If her mother had slept around, it would certainly explain her reluctance to tell Avery about her life here…but it was still almost impossible to believe. Winona wasn't that kind of woman! She wore necklines that covered her cleavage, and hemlines that skimmed her knees. She was careful not to be "overly friendly" with married men, lest someone think she was flirting. On the other hand, she did know an awful lot about how men worked…

"I see—" Avery tried to stem the rising tears. But a reputation was a very subjective thing, and perhaps Louis was more prudish than most. She'd known her mother had had a relationship at some point, because Avery was the result. Maybe Hope was just an old-fashioned little town whose population got easily scandalized. Maybe Louis was the kind of man who blamed the girl he got pregnant.

"But I liked her a lot," Louis added. "Your mom was a good person."

As if that made this better. He'd just called her loose. She'd been hoping to find a father who had at least loved her mother, even if they hadn't worked out. Winona had deserved to be loved.

I liked her a lot. That wasn't enough. There was a couple of beats of silence between them, and Louis put his hat back on his head.

"Were you one of the heartbroken guys?" Avery asked.

"Me?" He shook his head. "No, no… I knew where I stood. I was just some ranch boy. She had her eyes on the city."

"So…you and my mother weren't serious?" she pressed.

"Serious?" He shot her an odd look. "Sorry if I gave the wrong impression there. We were nothing more than good friends."

That was the story he was sticking with? They'd obviously been significantly more than good friends for a least one night, but it didn't look like he was going to admit to that—at least not today. Besides, her mind was whirling with this new bombshell he'd dropped on her, and she needed to process it alone.

"I'd better turn in." She hooked a thumb back toward the bunkhouse. "I've got an early morning."

"Look, I'm sorry to hear about your mom's passing," Louis said. "Real sorry."

"Thank you." She stood there awkwardly for a moment.

"Well, have a good night." He turned back toward his truck. "And welcome aboard."

Avery watched him go. If Louis wasn't willing to admit to even a casual relationship with her mom, then he might not be too pleased to discover that he'd fathered a child with her. What was it that he said, that some people grew and learned and let go of their mistakes? Somehow Avery doubted that she'd be welcome news. She might very well be one his mistakes that he gratefully set free. It would be wise to find out what she could about her biological family before courting rejection.

The next morning, Hank awoke at 3:30 a.m. and rolled over with a moan. He'd promised to give Avery a hand with breakfast, and though he was exhausted, he found himself grudgingly looking forward to it.

He tossed back his covers and sat up, rubbing his hands over his eyes. This house had had five years to be brought back down to a man's level, and all remnants of Vickie's touch around the place had been erased. He slept in the center of his bed, spread eagle. His bathroom contained soap, shaving gel, deodorant, a tooth-brush and shampoo—that was it. His bedroom was clean, but sparsely decorated, just the way he liked it. He had no reason to complicate his life with frills.

He flicked on the TV mounted on the wall opposite his bed as he ambled into the bathroom. He could hear the muffled voice of the news announcer talking about the weather. Mostly sunny, high of eighty, 20 percent chance of showers. The weather mattered on a ranch—rain mattered, heat mattered. There were eight hundred head of cattle that needed to be watered and cared for.

He washed his face and reached for his shaving gel. Sometimes he'd let his scruff go for a few days, but this morning a clean shave felt worth it. Fifteen min-utes later, he was dressed and he left the house, slam-ming the door shut behind him. He headed down the gravel drive that led to the canteen. Rocks crunched under his boots, and cool morning air carried the scent of cows and grass. The Harmon Ranch was home in a way that he'd never anticipated when he first took this job. Back then he'd been a young husband looking for a better wage—period—but he and Louis had forged a close relationship over the years through their per-sonal tragedies. He'd never expected the position to last longer than his marriage, but it had, and this familiar land, the cycle of the seasons, a warm, dark summer morning, felt safe.

The sun was beginning to warm the edge of the east-ern horizon, but all was still dark and quiet. The can-teen door was unlocked, which meant Avery was likely already in the kitchen. He locked the door behind him and saw light shining through the circular window of the swinging door.

"That you, Hank?" she called.

"Yeah, that's me." He walked into the kitchen.

She stood by the sink, tying an apron around her waist. She looked up as he came in.

"Morning," she said, a smile on her lips. Her hair was a little tousled, and she wasn't wearing any makeup—just that milky white skin and the red fringe of her lashes. "So what's the plan?"

"We have to put out thirty-five pack lunches," Hank said. "And get breakfast cooked. I can do the lunches." He opened a drawer and pulled out a box of hairnets. "You should probably use one of these."

That should make her a little less appealing to the guys.

"Of course." She flushed as she pulled her hair back, then twisted it into a bun at the base of her neck. "Give me a hand?"

He stretched out a hairnet and stepped closer so he could put it on her. She smelled good—that feminine mix of scents that a man never could identify. When he put the hairnet over her shining hair, his fingers brushed her neck. It had been a long time since he'd been this close to a woman, and he steeled himself to her softness, then took a step back.

"You'll probably want to start with corn bread," he said, trying to keep on task. "The old cook used to make it in batches—at least that's how he explained it to me before he left. The ovens hold eight pans at a time, and he did two batches..." He relayed what he'd been told, and showed her the recipe book. Avery gave him a quick nod.

She picked it up easily, which was a relief, because he wasn't sure he knew what he was doing, either. They needed to feed thirty-five men before they left for the fields, and that was a bigger job than he'd imagined. But they'd have food out there in an hour's time, and that was the goal. He worked on turkey sandwiches and cream cheese bagels, the results less than attractive but definitely edible.

"So tell me about you," she said as she cracked eggs into the mixing bowl.

"Not much to tell," he said.

"There's always something to tell," she replied. "Is your family from Hope?"

"Born and raised."

"You said your parents are in Florida now, right? Do you miss them?"

"I'm thirty-five," he said with a short laugh. "I'm a grown man."

"I didn't ask how old you were," she retorted. "I asked if you missed them."

Did he? Sometimes. But he could pick up a phone and call them whenever he wanted. They texted him pictures of geckos and potted cactus plants from their stone-covered yard. Not the life for him—he liked the fields, the cattle. When he retired, he wanted to own a little cabin somewhere with a fireplace and a dog.

"Sometimes," he admitted. "But we keep in touch."

"Shoot…" She dropped an eggshell on the table. "I've lost count and the yolks are broken. Okay, I'm quadrupling the batch—" She was silent for a moment, then continued, "No, I'm good… I think… We'll see."

What was it about her, standing there ruining a perfectly good meal—he could feel it happening, like lightning in the air—that she still managed to be so blasted likable?

"My mother always said a man expects a woman to be able to cook," she said, shooting him an amused look. "I'm a walking disappointment."

She fiddled with a few switches on the mixer until it turned on, the motor whirring softly as the large bowl turned.

"My ex-wife could cook like a pro," he said with a shrug. "And she was still impossible to live with."

He suppressed an oath. He hadn't meant to mention Vickie. That was personal, and this woman was a virtual stranger.

"What happened?" she asked, planting her hands on her hips while she watched the mixer spin.

"We grew apart."

That was the BS line most people used—the explanation that covered a hundred tiny betrayals before the ultimate one. Sometimes the ultimate betrayal wasn't even that big—it was just the last one before both parties gave up. No one just up and got divorced; they crept toward it at a snail's pace and pretended everything was fine until one day it wasn't.

"I don't believe that," Avery said, her tone unchanged. "My mom got divorced when I was seventeen, so I've seen it up close and personal. No one grows apart—they're pushed that way."

"And what was their problem?" he asked, trying to divert that attention away from his life. She seemed to like to talk, so it was better to focus it on her, in his opinion.

"He wanted to be the man of the house and call the shots," she said, reaching into the bowl with a spatula. "And he was terrible with money, but he wouldn't let her handle the finances because he was the man. She couldn't just watch him spend them into the poorhouse, and he couldn't just watch her take care of the banking. It was a no-win situation."

"Okay." She seemed to have a pretty good grasp on her mother's failed marriage.

"So what happened to yours?" she prompted.

She was turned away from him, focused on pouring flour into the mixing bowl. He didn't really mean to start talking about himself, but when he opened his mouth, it came out before he could think better of it.

"Vickie was more social than I was. She was a flirt, and I didn't like it. I loved horses and cattle, and she liked the Honky Tonk and dancing. There wasn't much overlap in our interests."

"That was it? Different interests?" She turned toward him, as if this really mattered to her.

"Well, that and Vickie thought that finally having a child together might solve our problems, and I'd disagreed. Babies bring more stress. They don't fix problems. Turns out not having a baby didn't fix it, either."

"That's a more honest answer." She smiled weakly. "Sorry. It must have been painful."

"Yeah, I got over it."

"How long ago was it?" she asked.

"Five years."

"I don't think you're over it," she said, flicking off the mixer. Her tone was so matter-of-fact that he nearly laughed.

"You don't know me," he retorted, stopping in mid-slice with a bagel. "How do you know what I'm over?"

"Are you married?" she asked. "Girlfriend? Fiancée?"

"No."

"You're good-looking, fit, technically available…" Her gaze moved over him from head to toe, then color suffused her cheeks. "If you were over her, you'd be snapped up."

She thought he was good-looking, did she? He liked that. And she had a bit of a point—he wasn't really available. He was no idealistic young cowpoke who thought love could conquer all. He was dusted up, scraped over and a little more cynical about the longevity of relationships. He and Vickie hadn't just split up, she'd left him for a guy she'd met online.

"How long were you married?" she asked.

"Twelve years. We got married right out of high school," he said.

"Ouch." She cast him a pitying look, and he scowled. He didn't need sympathy.

"So what about you?" he asked. "You said you didn't have anyone waiting for you."

"I was dating a guy," she said. "Can you reach those for me?"

Her change in topic was slightly jarring, and he looked over to see what she was referring to. There were some metal pans high on a shelf, and he put down the knife and sauntered over to where she stood. The soft scent of whatever perfume she was wearing tugged at him as he reached for the pans and handed them to her.

"Thanks," she said. "So I was dating a guy, but it didn't work out."

They stood facing each other, her chin tipped up so she could look him in the face. She was young, so much prettier than he could easily deflect. He felt old and disillusioned next to her. He felt like he should shut up, not ruin what was left of her innocence. She'd get to his position soon enough, and it was almost cruel to hurry that process. Or maybe she wouldn't. Maybe she'd marry some guy who would adore her and let her take care of the finances.

"So what went wrong?" he asked. "And you can't use *we grew apart*."

"He wasn't the right one," she said. She made it sound so simple and obvious, but he doubted that the guy who lost her felt that way. He had a feeling the poor schmuck was probably still licking his wounds, wondering what went wrong. She turned away from him and headed toward the side-by-side stoves. She turned a couple of dials, opened the ovens, stuck a hand in.

"I think that's turned on," she said.

"So how did you know he wasn't right?" Hank asked. "What line did you give him?"

"He wanted me to sell the flower shop," she said, her back to him. "And if he knew me at all, he would have known that store meant more to me than money."

Avery turned around to face him, meeting his eyes with her frank gaze.

"How recently was this?" he asked

"Last month."

Avery picked up the first pan of corn bread and slid it into the oven.

"The oven isn't on," he said.

"What? No, I just—" She put her hand into the oven again, then frowned.

He stepped up to the stove and turned the correct dial, then flicked the oven switch. Color tinged her cheeks.

"And that's what you told him?" he asked, letting her mistake go. "That he didn't know you well enough?" Why was he so curious about her breakup? For some reason, he needed to know what the poor guy had been through.

"I said it wasn't him, it was me. And it wasn't his fault. Not really. That store is my home."

"I get it," Hank said. It was like his connection to the land and the cattle. Vickie had never been able to understand that it wasn't a choice. The open range just kept tugging him back. Home was something hardwired inside a person, something that called and called, no matter how hard a man tried to walk away. Home trumped logic. It could be ignored for a time, pushed aside for a while, but it couldn't be denied forever—not even for the strongest principles. In his opinion, it wasn't growing apart that ended a couple. It was starting out apart and never growing together.

Somewhere in Kansas there was another guy nursing a broken heart, and Hank felt a strange camaraderie with the man. They were like soldiers who'd served in the same war, or survivors who'd gone through the same tornado. There was some unspoken bond between men who'd been through the wringer.

Women were complicated, and Avery looked more so than the rest. What did that say about his morbid curiosity that he still wanted to figure Avery out?

Chapter Four

Avery looked down into the blackened bottom of the oatmeal pot. Granted, she'd never made oatmeal in such a large quantity before, but she really hadn't expected to mess it up. Even with milk and brown sugar, it tasted rather smoky.

The corn bread had turned out a little dense, but surprisingly tasty. The eight dozen boiled eggs had gone over well, as had the bacon—she couldn't fry it up fast enough for the hungry men. By the time they were finished eating, she'd been exhausted.

Avery gathered some empty serving trays and backed up against the swinging door that led to the kitchen. The men were donning hats once more and heading out. Hank stood on the far side the room, his gaze fixed on her.

Had she done well? It was better than last night's supper. She let the kitchen door swing shut behind her and carried the crumb-laden trays to the counter. She put them down with a clatter and heaved a sigh.

Hank poked his head into the kitchen just as she was turning back for her second trip.

"Not bad," he said.

"Except for the oatmeal," she replied with a grimace. "Sorry about that."

"Yeah… We'll work on that."

At least she wasn't fired—that was something. And it was an improvement over the stew. Hank had left her a schedule for what to cook when, and tonight's menu was chili, biscuits and baked potatoes. Fingers crossed for that one.

"I can't stay here today—duty calls. So you're on your own," Hank said, then he paused, shot her a questioning look.

"I'll be fine," she said. "I actually make a very good chili."

Hers was from a can, but she did add in extra beef and some chunky vegetables…and she'd been complimented on it, too. And while she wouldn't have forty cans of chili to start her off, she would have some online recipes. And most of the day to figure things out.

"If you need me…" He didn't have to finish that. She had his cell number.

"I'll be fine."

She didn't feel quite as confident as she sounded, but with the odd looks she got from Hank when she checked out YouTube tutorials, maybe being on her own would be easier.

"Okay," he said, giving her a curt nod. "See you later."

Hank disappeared behind the swinging door, and just for a moment, she wished she had an excuse to call him back. Hank was the closest thing she had to

a friend here on her father's ranch…and she liked his
company. He didn't smile quickly or easily, but when
he did, she felt like she'd achieved something. He was
serious and self-contained—an open challenge to her
more outgoing personality. She was curious about his
life, too—what forces had created the solemn cowboy?
But Hank wasn't here to hold her hand, no matter how
nice it might be to have a rugged cowboy fixing that
intense gaze on her all day long. She blushed at the
thought. Hank was good-looking, but it was more than
lanky height and clear blue eyes…he had the air of a
man who was experienced in life, and while she knew
she had no business meddling with him, it did make
her take notice.

You're too young for him to take you seriously. She
could hear what her mother would say in that place in
the back of her mind where Winona's voice would always live. *Don't lose your heart to a man who isn't
losing his.*

Had her mother made that mistake with Louis?
Avery wished she knew.

Avery looked around the kitchen at the dirty pots,
the plastic bins full of plates and bowls. The major-
ity of this job would be the cleaning up, she could already tell. But she wasn't actually here to be a cook.
She'd have to find a way to cross paths with her father
if she was going to make good use of this time. From
what she could see of the ranch, Louis was a prosper-
ous man. His employees ate well, and they all seemed
happy enough to be working here, so she could assume
they were paid decently, too.

Avery hadn't had much growing up. Her mother worked hard, and they lived in a small apartment above the flower shop that was technically a one-bedroom place, but her mother had artfully transformed a walk-in closet to be a second bedroom for Avery. They hadn't traveled much, except for one trip to Disneyland when Avery was about ten. Her mother had saved for years to make it happen, and when she received a small inheritance from an aunt, they'd packed their bags for the only vacation that Avery and her mother would ever take together.

And all that time, her father was running a ranch with cattle and barns, ranch hands and horses… Had her father known about her mother's pregnancy but hadn't wanted to be involved? It was possible. Maybe he was an accomplished liar, though he didn't seem the type. But if he hadn't known about Avery's existence, that meant her mother had simply denied her daughter a relationship with her father and the financial stability that would have come with it.

She hadn't decided what she felt about all this yet. Her mother never did anything without good reason, and that included the little things like buying candy along with the groceries or getting a new pair of shoes. Everything had to be rationalized. She could still remember her mother's voice. "You haven't outgrown your last pair of runners, but you will soon. So I'll get you this new pair, but they have to be a size bigger so that they'll last. Or we could wait… But the sale is on now, and I don't want to miss out on that…"

If there had been a father who could have sent money

for school clothes, or even provided them a vacation once every couple of years…that would have made a big difference. So why would her mother have kept Avery away from her dad?

She heard movement behind her and turned to see a teenage girl standing in the doorway. There were still a few men exiting the building, and she could hear their voices suddenly drop off as the outside door banged shut. The teenager was slim and tanned with dark hair and gray eyes that were disconcertingly light compared to her dark complexion.

"Hi," Avery said.

"I'm Olivia Harmon," the girl said, crossing the kitchen and holding out her hand. Avery's heart sped up at the young woman's name. Her sister. They looked nothing alike, but genetics could be like that. She wiped her palms on her apron and shook Olivia's proffered hand.

"Nice to meet you. I'm the new cook."

"I heard." Olivia put her fingers into her back pockets and looked around. "I just came by to pick up a couple of pack lunches for Dad and me."

"Going out together?" Avery asked, trying to sound casual.

"Yeah, we're going riding." Olivia headed to the large refrigerator and pulled it open. "Aren't there any left?"

"I don't think so. Hank made an even thirty-five this morning," Avery said. "Do you want me to make you a couple of lunches?"

"Don't worry about it," Olivia said. "I can do it. I won't keep you from whatever you were doing."

The dishes—that was what Avery had been doing. She had the big sink filled with hot, soapy water, and she pulled on a pair of rubber gloves.

"That's nice that your dad goes riding with you," Avery said as she grabbed a scrub brush and got to work.

"Yeah, we've been riding together since I was little." Olivia pulled sandwich fixings from the fridge. "He's actually heading out to check on some leaking pipes that are being fixed, and I'm tagging along."

"How old are you?" Avery asked.

"Sixteen. Why?"

"You look older than that," Avery said quickly. "You could pass for nineteen easily." What teenager didn't want to look older than her years? That might cover up any weird-sounding curiosity on Avery's part.

"How about twenty-one?" Olivia asked with a grin.

"Not quite." Avery chuckled. She wasn't about to encourage anything untoward.

"Why, how old are you?" Olivia asked. Only a teenager would ask a grown woman that question and not bat an eye.

"Twenty-four," Avery said. "So very, very old."

"Only moderately," Olivia said and Avery laughed. "Uncle Hank says that you might not stay too long?"

"No, I—" Avery wondered how much to say. Eventually, Olivia would know who she was, but she couldn't guarantee the girl would like it. She didn't want to be telling any lies when she'd be telling them the whole truth soon enough. "My mom passed away a little while ago, and I'm going to have to go back and run her flower shop."

"Oh…" Olivia nodded. "My mom died a couple of years ago, too. It's hard. I'm sorry."

"Thanks." For some reason, this girl's sympathy was comforting. She dropped the scrub brush and pulled down her rubber glove to expose a bracelet. "Mom gave me this years ago. I still wear it everywhere. It reminds me of her."

Olivia crossed the kitchen to take a closer look. She cocked her head to one side, reading the inscription on the silver bangle.

"'Home is where the heart is…'" Olivia read aloud.

"It isn't terribly unique," Avery admitted. "She got it from one of those gift catalogues that schools use for fund-raising. But she said that no matter where we were, as long as we were together, that was home."

The memory brought tears to her eyes. When they found themselves in long lineups, or in the fragrant warehouse where they picked up their order of flowers for the store, they'd remind each other that home was where the heart was, and in the most literal sense possible…it was right where they stood.

Home, sweet home, her mother would say, and she'd shoot Avery one of those private smiles. And nowhere felt more like home than inside Winona's Wilderness.

"Nice," Olivia said with a nod. She pulled her dark hair away from her ears and pushed forward some diamond studs. "These belonged to my mom."

"Pretty," Avery said. "It's nice to have a reminder of her, isn't it?"

"Yeah."

They exchanged a smile, then Olivia headed back to the counter where she was assembling the lunches. It was good to bond with the girl over something real. They'd both lost their mothers, and while Avery had lost hers when she was a grown woman, she guessed that the hole left behind would be the same at any age.

"My dad isn't available, though," Olivia added, her attention riveted to the job in front of her.

"Available for what?" Avery asked, pulling a dripping pot out of the water. She squeezed the nozzle and shot hot water over it, rinsing off the soap.

"You know…dating. Women. That kind of thing."

"Oh!" Avery looked over her shoulder again. "Do you think I'm coming on to your dad or something? I can promise you that I have no interest in your father in that way—"

"No, no…" Olivia laughed self-consciously. "It's just that Uncle Hank said…"

"Said what?" Avery asked. Hank had been discussing her with her father's kids?

"Just that he thought you might be interested in Dad, that's all."

That was both irritating and alarming. She'd thought she'd kept her secret pretty well, but to have him assume that she was after Louis for romance… It was even more angering to think that he'd been talking behind her back about it, too. She was an employee here, and while she *had* taken the job for her own reasons, she knew her rights.

"Tell *Uncle Hank* that he's got it wrong," Avery said drily.

"Don't tell him I said anything." Olivia tossed the lunches into a bag. "It wasn't like he was complaining or anything. We were just talking about you—"

"Yeah?" Avery stayed focused on the dishes in front of her. "What about me?"

"That you're pretty, that's all. Nothing to get offended over." The fridge door shut and Olivia's footfalls moved toward the exit.

"I've got to go," Olivia said. "Nice to meet you, though. See you!"

And with that, Olivia headed out the swinging doors. Avery hadn't meant to scare the girl off, but then, Olivia hadn't intended to stay and chat. She looked out the window, the wrong side of the building to see anything.

That's my sister. The thought was still settling in as she stood there by the sudsy sink. She had two siblings, and she wondered how they'd feel about finding out their father had sired her almost a decade before they were born. Would they be angry? Would they be glad to know her? Sixteen-year-olds weren't known for their emotional maturity in these kinds of situations. Olivia's worry seemed to be that she'd want to sink her claws into Louis, but that couldn't be further from the truth. Except, she did want *something* from Louis...

Avery could see a turn of dusty road, and two riders came into view for just a moment. Louis and Olivia were headed out on their father-daughter ride. They rode easily side by side. Louis appeared to say something, and Olivia laughed. Then they were out of sight again.

Avery hadn't come for romance or inheritance. In fact, when she'd planned this, she thought that she only wanted to meet her father…let him know that she existed. But now that she could see what she'd missed out on, she realized that deep down she wanted more than a simple acknowledgment. She'd spent twenty-four years without a dad, and she could feel the injustice of that as she thought about her father with the daughter he knew about. Avery wanted more than to announce her presence, she wanted what Olivia had with their father—a relationship.

HANK PULLED OFF his work gloves and headed over to the fence where Mr. Harmon stood with two horses. It was only the second week of June, but they had summer heat already. It would be a warmer year than usual. They could only hope that wouldn't contribute to a drought. The sun beat down on his shoulders, and sweat trickled down his spine. The men were working on a sprinkler system that had lost water pressure, and Olivia peered over shoulders, watching the work up close. That was a good thing—she'd own this ranch one day, or at least half of it, and she'd need to know how everything was done. Saturdays on the ranch with her dad she learned just as much as she did Mondays in school. If not more.

"How's it going?" his boss asked.

"Found the leak. We'll be done soon. Hopefully this is the last one."

Mr. Harmon nodded, pursing his lips. His practiced gaze moved over the workers. "How's the cook?"

"She's—" What could he truthfully say? She was a warm body filling a position, but she wasn't any good at it. "She's trying real hard."

"The guys can't live on burned food, no matter how pretty the cook," Mr. Harmon said, his voice low. "Now, I know she isn't long-term, but I don't want to start losing experienced help because the food is awful, either."

"I hear you," Hank agreed. His boss was right. A ranch was only as successful as the men who worked it. And if they lost qualified, experienced workers, everything would suffer. The Harmons had always been good to their employees, and the older rancher had a reputation around here that made his operation one of the most desirable places to work. Louis wasn't going to want to toy with that—even for someone as pretty as Avery.

"The other problem is that I've been hearing how the men are talking about her." Mr. Harmon's expression was unimpressed. "First of all, I don't want her harassed."

Olivia stood not far off, and Hank could tell she was listening. He agreed—women needed to be treated with respect around here.

"Of course. I'm on it," Hank said.

"And second, you know my policy about employees dating. Granted, it's never been much of a problem because we don't tend to have many women working here, but I can see that it might be an issue now."

Mr. Harmon gave Hank a level look, and Hank resisted the urge to shift his feet. He'd found their new cook quite alluring, too, but Louis didn't have to worry about him. He had too much to lose here to risk it all on a cute cook.

"The policy is what it's always been," Hank replied. "Any staff caught fraternizing are let go. Period."

He nodded slowly, then pulled out his handkerchief and mopped the back of his neck.

"Do the guys have it under control here?" his boss asked.

"Yeah, they're set."

"Good. I want you to head back to the kitchen and make sure that at least one meal comes out fully edible. If she can't pull it together soon, I'm going to have to let her go, anyway."

Professionally, Hank couldn't argue with that. A cook wasn't much use to anyone if she couldn't do her job. It shouldn't matter to him—she was a complete stranger who'd dropped into their laps and sparked his suspicions early on. He should be glad to see the back of her…but he didn't like the idea of Avery being let go.

"Let me see what I can do," Hank said with a sigh. "About all of it."

Hank stopped by the workers to make sure they had their last instructions, then headed toward his vehicle on the side of the road about a hundred yards off. The day was already hot, and it wasn't yet noon. By the time five rolled around, the men would be hungry, thirsty and exhausted. Their patience would start wearing thin if they didn't get a decent meal soon.

Avery was a terrible cook. She showed up on time,

she worked hard and she cared, but she lacked the basic kitchen skills to put out a meal that people could eat. If Mr. Harmon let her go, the cooking would fall to Hank until they could find someone better. He didn't want to go shorthanded while one of the other ranch hands worked the kitchen, and Hank had no intention of being stuck in there all day, either. The Harmon ranch had very little fat to pinch, something in which Hank took personal pride. He was the manager, and keeping this place humming without too much waste was his responsibility. Besides, while he should be just as happy to be rid of a potential problem, he was loath to see her go. She made life around here a little more interesting.

Hank hopped in his truck and looked over his shoulder to where the work was being done. Mr. Harmon looked in his direction once, and raised his hand in a wave. The boss had been clear enough about what he wanted, and Avery probably deserved to hear the truth—most of it, at least. If she wanted to keep this job, then they had some work to do.

Hank drove up the winding gravel road to the canteen. He normally liked this drive, where the countryside spilled out in front of him in rolling hills and the straight lines of the fields. He liked to listen to the radio on low and breathe in the scent of grass. But today, he was frustrated. If he didn't find a way to improve Avery's cooking, then she'd be canned, and that was the thought that stayed prominent as he drove up toward the low, wide bunkhouse.

He wasn't supposed to care—not on a personal level, at least—but he was getting attached to her, despite his better judgment. Had it been that long since he'd had some female company? It wasn't just that she was attractive, either. He liked listening to her talk, and he talked around her a whole lot more than he ever intended to. Was this something riskier that he should get control of now?

He parked out front and hopped out of his truck, ambling into the cool dimness of the canteen. All was silent and still. Was she even here? He angled around the tables and pushed open the swinging kitchen door.

Avery stood with her back to him. Her hair was up in the hairnet, except for one curling tendril that fell down her pale neck. She was looking at something in front of her, and he could just make out the tinny voice of a cooking show.

"...add the lemon zest, garlic and hot pepper to the oil, making sure to keep the mixture moving so it doesn't cook too quickly..."

She was watching one of her YouTube videos.

He leaned against the door frame, watching her for a moment. She didn't hear him, but she slowly turned, her gaze still fixed on her phone, and he wished in this moment that she were a little plainer. Bossing her around would be a whole lot easier if he weren't constantly fighting his own instincts to soften his tone, be a little kinder, make her like him. What should it matter if she liked him or not, as long as she respected him as her boss?

"Howdy," he said, and she startled, dropping her phone with a clatter.

"You scared me!" she gasped, then started looking

around for the phone. Hank bent down and retrieved it—unbroken, thankfully.

"Sorry," he said. "We need to talk."

"I was just about to start the chili," she said. "What's going on?"

He could try to sugarcoat this, or he could just tell her straight. "Mr. Harmon needs you to cook a decent meal, or he'll let you go."

Hank handed her phone back, and she accepted it with a small frown.

"He said that?"

"Yes."

"But breakfast was good…all but the oatmeal."

"He needs a meal where nothing is burned. His words." Hank watched her for a reaction but got nothing more than a sigh. "So I'm here to help you out."

"Really?" She looked up, green-flecked eyes meeting his hopefully. "I thought you'd be busy with other things."

"I was." And for all his irritation about being sent back for such a menial task, he was grudgingly glad to be here with her. Frankly, any of the other guys would have given much anything to be stuck alone with the cook for a few hours, and here he was.

"Thank you, Hank." His name sounded nice on her tongue. He grunted in response. "I really mean it."

"You're cooking for a large group of ranch hands," Hank said, nodding toward her phone. "No lemon zest. Nothing fancy. That pot that you filled for oatmeal needs to be filled with chili by the time we're done today. And we're working with the basics."

"Okay." She tucked her phone back into her pocket. "This recipe called for red wine, too, so—"

He eyed her, waiting to see if she was joking. She met his gaze evenly, no hint of humor. He smothered a sigh.

"You realize your job is on the line here," he clarified.

She didn't answer him, but she crossed her arms under her breasts and her expression changed to something slightly less cooperative.

"Go get the recipe binder I gave you," Hank ordered, heading to the pantry. He grabbed a couple of heads of garlic and four onions, depositing them on the center island just as she came back with the recipe he'd requested.

"So you'll be helping me?" she asked.

"Nope," he replied. "I'll be telling you what to do. Today, you're learning the ropes."

"Oh." She nodded. "Fair enough."

"Get the pot on the stove and turn it on," he commanded. "What does the recipe call for?"

She scanned the page. "Oil, garlic, onions and hot peppers."

"Okay, then." He nodded toward the cutting board already on the island. "Get chopping."

"You're bossy," she muttered, but she did as he ordered and started with the garlic first.

"You have no idea," he replied, crossing his arms. "What about the pot?"

"You said to—" She sighed, then fetched the pot and plunked it on the stove. She leaned forward and turned it on.

"We're starting with the chili because it will take longest," he said.

"I know *that*, Hank," she retorted. "I'm sorry that things haven't gone perfectly lately, but it isn't because I'm a half-wit." She used the flat of the knife to press the garlic and pulled the skins off. Then she started to mince it.

"I never once called you a half-wit," he replied with small smile. "Cooking isn't linked with intelligence."

"Oh, and what is it linked to?" she retorted.

He was liking this irritated, glistening Avery. She was pretty when she was happy, but angry she was downright gorgeous. That age gap seemed to lessen when she challenged him, too.

"Cooking is linked to passion," he said, shooting her a teasing smile.

"So, if I'm such a miserable cook, why does rumor have it that you think I'm here to seduce Mr. Harmon?"

Hank nearly choked. "What? Who said that?"

It was true, but he'd thought he'd been discreet about his suspicions.

"Word gets around," she said, shooting him an arch look. "Should we set that one to rest right now? First of all, I have no interest in starting up any romantic relationships while I'm in Hope, and second, I'm not interested in older men. So you can let your guard down. You may find cause to fire me, but it won't be for that."

Older men. That included him, he realized, and he didn't find it disappointing as much as challenging. She wasn't interested? Give him some time…

Then he stopped himself. He wasn't about to get himself fired, either.

"I'm not accusing you of anything," he countered.

"Not to my face," she replied. "Look, Hank, you're my boss. And I have no problems with authority, but I do have a few problems with having my reputation smeared behind my back."

Avery grabbed the next bulb of garlic and set to work on it, her knife hitting the cutting board with solid thunks—definitely harder than necessary.

"Avery—" He had to raise his voice to get her attention, and she stopped, looked up at him with eyebrows raised. "I'm sorry. You seemed overly interested in the boss. That's all. You'll have to forgive me for looking out for him. But if you say you aren't interested in him, then I'll take your word."

And she did seem to be honestly indignant at the thought, so maybe she was telling the truth and she was here for some other reason. She finished with the garlic and reached for the first onion.

"Now, do you want my help today, or not?" he asked.

Avery paused in her chopping, pink rising in her cheeks. "I'd like your help," she said, and then after a pause added, "please."

"Okay." He tempered his tone. "And maybe I could be nicer."

She didn't quite smile, but her expression softened. "I'd like that."

Blast, and all of a sudden he realized that her soft voice held more power than he'd imagined. Hank's bark was worse than his bite, but it did cover all those pesky emotions that got in the way.

He was keeping her from getting fired, and that was all. He'd best remember that.

Chapter Five

Avery was relieved at how well dinner turned out. The chili was slightly bland, but not burned and very edible. The baked potatoes were easy enough, and while they weren't piping hot when served, the toppings made up the difference. She was still pulling biscuits out of the oven the entire time the men were eating—she hadn't timed that right—but all in all the meal was a success, and Avery's job was saved for another day. She felt triumphant—a battle won. *Learn how to cook or let 'em down easy* had been her mother's advice, and in this job, she didn't really get the second option. The men had been enthusiastic and she'd received several compliments on the meal, which did a lot for her confidence in her abilities. It was possible that she wasn't as bad of a cook as she thought.

With Hank's help, of course. He'd stayed true to his word and stopped ordering her around. Cooking with him had actually been fun after that. She'd managed to get him talking a little bit—which cut down on the bossing around—and he'd told her about some of the workers and a few funny stories around the ranch. He'd stayed by the pot of chili and kept stirring so it wouldn't burn, and every once in a while, she'd look up from whatever she was doing and find his gaze on her. He'd look away when she caught him. Why was he watching her so much?

Hank left the kitchen once the meal was served, ate with the guys and then headed out without stopping in to say goodbye. Was that a positive sign? Was this meal going to pass muster with Louis?

The next couple of days were the same. Hank came by to help her cook, and while they worked, they talked. He seemed more friendly, and with each meal they were able to work together more and more seamlessly. Except she was supposed to do this job alone, and Hank was wasting his time in the kitchen with her.

Two days later, by the time she'd finished the supper cleanup, the sun was low in the sky. Hank had left after the meal, having other duties that needed his attention. As far as she could tell, the man was working a job and a half in helping her to do hers, so she didn't mind cleaning up alone.

Avery thought idly about the fact that her own father was considering firing her. He didn't know he was her father, and somehow that made it worse. She'd applied for the job as a way to connect with her dad, and so far, she hadn't succeeded in that. She'd underestimated those professional boundaries. She'd seen a whole lot more of Hank than she had of Louis, and this job was pointless if it didn't allow her a chance to see her father. While he was never more than a mile away, she'd only managed to have one conversation with him so far.

Avery took off her apron and hairnet and hung them

on a hook. She flicked the lights off behind her and headed out through the seating area toward the front door. The evening was cool. She paused, listening to the twitter of birds and enjoying the pink-and-orange sky. Was it crazy that she was starting to like it here?

Yes, it was crazy. Montana ranch land might be beautiful, but it wasn't home, and enjoying her father's land too much felt like a betrayal to her mother. She touched the bracelet on her wrist.

Avery had been thinking about her own childhood lately in relation to her father, and how different it might have been if he'd been a part of her life. But how might that have affected her mother? Winona would have been a lot more financially comfortable, too, so she must have kept her distance for a reason. Obviously, Louis hadn't thought too much of her mom if his way of describing her was *looking for love in all the wrong places*. Avery knew what that translated to, and frankly, she found it hypocritical for a man to judge a woman's behavior when he'd been the one who got her pregnant.

If Louis knew that she was his daughter, would it change anything? Maybe if they could talk a little, it would make revealing who she was easier. He was obviously a good father to the twins, and from what she'd pieced together, he'd been a devoted husband to his late wife. He was capable of being a dad…but was he willing to take on another child, even a grown one? Because she had less than two weeks before she let them off the hook in eating her cooking. She had to get home soon, so time was of the essence.

The Harmon house was up the road, and she decided

to walk. It was a quiet evening, with a refreshing breeze that pushed her hair away from her face. The sun was just a small crescent still visible above the horizon, the sky awash in coral pink and crimson suffusing the skyline. Twilight was the hardest time of day since her mother's passing. There was something about the not-quite-dark that made the jumble of emotions inside her that much clearer and harder to avoid.

I miss you, Mom.

If it weren't for the cancer, she'd be able to ask her mother all the questions, but then, her mom wouldn't have given her Louis's name, either. Winona hadn't wanted Avery to contact Louis—certainly not in her lifetime.

As her shoes crunched over the gravel, she wondered what she could realistically expect from the man. Maybe embracing her as part of his family was a long shot, but she wanted him to know that she existed at the very least. Then if he closed off, she'd know her mother had been right.

The walk between the canteen and the house was a good fifteen minutes, and the fresh air helped to untangle her nerves. As she approached, she could see the curtains were open and the lights were on, giving her a clear view into the sitting room. She saw the back of a chair, a painting on the opposite wall. Louis's son, Owen, passed in front of the window, a book or a phone in his hands that occupied his attention. At least she assumed the teenage boy was Owen. She searched her heart for some emotion. That was her brother... She didn't know what that was supposed to feel like.

The side door opened and Hank stepped out. She could see his face in the light that flooded out from the kitchen, and she recognized his shoulders and the way he held himself. The rumble of low voices carried over to her as Louis and Hank exchanged a few words, and then the door closed again and Hank pushed his hands into his pockets and started walking in her direction.

She froze. Had he seen her? She didn't have a plan, exactly. She thought she might knock on the door and ask some questions about the kitchen or something... make an excuse to talk to Louis a little bit. But with Hank coming straight at her, she was reminded of what he thought her intentions toward Louis were, and she didn't want to play into that image.

"Evening." Hank's voice was low, but not unfriendly. "What are you doing out here?"

"Just taking a walk."

Hank stopped close to her, his eyes shining in the low light. "Dinner was good tonight."

"Thanks to you." She could feel his body heat, and she realized she was a little chilly. "Is... Did Mr. Harmon mention me at all?"

"Your job is safe," Hank replied. "He's not unfair. He just wants to make sure that his guys are getting fed properly, that's all. He has nothing personal against you."

Nothing personal... They had no idea. "That's good."

He was silent for a moment, regarding her. "So...just walking around at night, then?"

She looked toward the house once more and suppressed a sigh. Maybe the timing wasn't right tonight, anyway.

"Clearing my head," she said with a small smile.

"It's pretty quiet around here," he said. "But we've been known to get a few coyotes. Also there are some wolves in the area that have been getting braver lately. They've been snatching calves. We guard the herds, but they come in pretty close some nights, and wandering around on your own isn't a great idea."

Avery shivered.

"I didn't know that," she admitted with a soft laugh.

"Care for some company?" he asked.

"Well, you do put up a fairly convincing argument not to be alone," she replied and he chuckled.

"I'll walk you back."

Avery had to admit that having this big man next to her was comforting, especially when she now knew what could lurk in the darkness. The ranch looked different at dusk. She could make out the headlights of a truck bouncing along a road in the distance, and there were dots on the hills that would be the cattle. The moon hadn't risen yet.

"It's darker than I thought," Avery said.

"See?" He sounded mildly glad to have her confirm it. "It's not like town where you can barely see the stars at night. It gets good and dark."

Her foot went into a shallow hole in the road, and she let out a breath of surprise.

"You okay?"

"Didn't see that." She was feeling a little dumb now for her decision to come walking at this time of night.

"Wait—so if you knew it was going to be so dark… what about your truck?"

"The boss was going to drive me back. I saw you out the window."

That was fair enough, but Louis could have driven them both back. Was Hank still trying to keep her away from his boss?

"The moon will come up soon." He held out his hand. "But this will make it easier not to trip."

"I'm feeling stupid," she admitted.

"Don't." His warm fingers closed down on her hand, and he tugged her close against his side. "I know all the potholes."

She laughed softly, and she had to admit that it wasn't so bad to be next to him. He smelled good—musky with a hint of hay. His grip was firm and strong, and when he tugged to one side, she found herself easily side-stepping another dip in the road. This wasn't the most professional situation, but she didn't mind. She wasn't here to grow her career, anyway.

"Wouldn't this look bad if anyone saw us?" she asked with a low laugh.

"Probably," he said.

"And we'd both find ourselves fired?" she clarified.

"If we were in a romantic relationship," he said. "I'm just getting you back in one piece."

She felt her cheeks flush, and she was glad for the veil of darkness. She wasn't a schoolgirl who now thought Hank was her boyfriend for holding her hand, but…it wouldn't look good, especially for a ranch with such strict rules.

"So why are you here?" he asked.

"You keep asking me that."

"Because you obviously aren't a cook."

She was silent for a moment, considering her options. "I don't think I know you well enough for this conversation," she admitted at last, and in response she heard a chuckle.

"Alright then...any brothers or sisters?" Hank asked.

"What are you doing?" she asked.

"You don't talk much about your family. I'm curious."

"You think it's your business?" she countered.

"I'm the ranch manager. Everything's my business."

"Even me?"

"Especially you." He looked down at her quizzically. "I'll figure you out yet, Miss Southerly."

And yet, here he was holding her hand on a dark night, and his voice sounded comforting and warm.

"No brothers or sisters. Just me," she said, relenting. "How about you?"

"Four sisters. All married. All with kids." She could hear the tension between the lines there.

"Is that four sisters intent on setting you up with someone?" she asked.

"Yes... Well, they might have lost some of their steam lately. I've been remarkably stubborn in that department."

"How come?" she asked.

"Because I've been there before—married and divorced. Not willing to do it again."

His grip on her hand tightened, and he stopped in his tracks.

"What's the matter?" she whispered.

"Shh." His arm tensed, the biceps hardening against her cheek.

Avery's heart hammered in her throat. She held her breath, listening, then looked around in one quick swivel. What had he seen? A wolf?

"Don't…move…" he ordered.

HANK SAW THEM coming out of the grass at the side of the road, waddling out onto the gravel. He might not have noticed them were it not for the white stripes down their backs. A mother skunk and three kits.

"What—" she began, and he squeezed her hand again. Then he heard her exhale. There it was—she'd seen them, too. The trick with skunks was not to scare them. A scared skunk would spray, a happy skunk would not. They were also a remarkably nearsighted animal with a hair-trigger defence system.

The skunks wandered closer, the mother first and the babies close behind. Avery started to move and he dropped her hand to slip his arm around her waist, pulling her firmly against his side. He could feel the rise and fall of her ribs against his hand. Her head came up to his shoulder and he could make out the faint fruity scent of her shampoo. If he could just keep her still for another minute…

"Don't move," he repeated softly, and when he felt her relax slightly, he loosened his grip. The woman in his arms was diverting his attention away from the skunks. He couldn't help but notice the way she felt— warm, firm, and he could feel the beat of her heart.

The skunks lost interest in their footwear and waddled off a few feet. Hank scooped up Avery's hand again and tugged her with him, slowly backing away. When they'd made a wide enough distance between them and the skunks, he let out a breath of relief.

"Oh, my goodness..." Avery laughed softly. "I thought there was a wolf or something."

"Ever been sprayed?" he asked wryly.

"No."

"I have. Trust me, you don't want to scare a skunk."

"So I suppose I should be glad of the personal escort." Her eyes glittered in the darkness, and he wasn't entirely sure if she was joking or not. There were dangers out there that she had no idea about.

"Let's get you back." He didn't let go of her hand, though, and she fell into step beside him.

When was the last time he'd held a woman's hand... for any reason? He'd taken a few women out for dinner over the last couple of years, but it hadn't gone much further than a first date. This was probably the most physical contact he'd had with a woman since his divorce, and this was supposed to be practical—just getting her back to her room in the dark. But his body was reacting like a whole lot more was going on, and he was noticing things about her, like the softness of her skin against his, the scent of her, the sound of her breath as she hurried to keep up with his long stride. He slowed a little.

"You said that you won't let your sisters set you up?" Avery asked.

"You don't get derailed from a conversation very easily, do you?" he asked with a low laugh.

"I guess not," she replied. "So how come?"

"You're young and idealistic. I'm not."

"Who says I'm idealistic?" she asked. "I watched my mother get divorced."

"Alright." He could make out the light from the windows of the bunkhouse now. "But you are young…and that makes a difference."

"Maybe it does," she agreed.

And he wished she'd been willing to fight with him a little bit over that one instead of agreeing so easily. Not that it mattered. He'd met Vickie when he was young and romantic. He used to write love poetry, for crying out loud. Terrible, rhyming love poetry that made him grimace even to remember it.

"Have you always been so bossy?" she asked after a moment of silence.

"What?" He looked down at her.

"You. You're bossy." She peered up at him, and again, he wasn't exactly sure how serious she was.

"I'm not… I'm just your boss." He gave her a quick smile.

She laughed at that. "You like giving orders. Being in control."

"Someone has to."

"I'm just saying, it's off-putting," she said.

Was it? It wasn't like he was like this with women he wanted to date. He was like this at work, and speaking of which, she was supposed to be his subordinate. But then again, they were holding hands. He let go of her. If she went into a pothole, she'd survive.

"I'm still your boss," Hank reminded her. "And I saved you from rabid skunks."

"They weren't rabid," Avery said with a laugh.

"Fine. Skunks, all the same."

"I will give you that. And you saved my job."

"See? Bossy isn't so bad."

What did she even want from him? He wasn't sure, and she wasn't asking. The moon came out from behind a cloud and they were suddenly illuminated in silver light. He cleared his throat and stepped back.

"Is that why you don't date?" she asked.

"Why do you care?"

"I'm not sure." He could hear the honesty in her tone. "I guess I like you."

As a person, or as more? It had been a long time since he'd talked with a woman like this—a little flirtatiously, no intentions whatsoever...

"Fine." Hank slowed his pace. They were getting close to the bunkhouse now, and he glanced toward it, then back to her upturned face. "I don't date because I don't want to fall in love again. My wife broke my heart. Besides, I like my life the way it is. I know that most women want the wedding. Can't say I blame them, but I've already done it. So I keep things uncomplicated."

"Oh." Avery was silent for a beat, then said, "You're right, though. I know I want a wedding."

"Even after your mother's miserable luck?" he asked.

"Yes." She shrugged faintly. "I believe in something bigger than luck."

He smiled at that. A breeze picked up, blowing her hair over her face, and she ran a finger through her curls, pulling them back. She was beautiful in the moonlight, her skin glowing pale with the scattering of freckles over her nose and down her cheeks. She had the kind of beauty that made a man's rational thoughts drain from his head, made him want to do things that he should know weren't good for him or his career... There was one red strand stuck to the moisture on her lip, and he reached forward and pulled it free. Those lips... They parted as she inhaled, and his gaze moved back up to her eyes.

This was where he was supposed to walk away, but he couldn't bring himself to do it, and for the first time, looking down into those clear eyes, he was positive that she wasn't joking.

"What's bigger than luck?" Hank asked softly.

"Love."

He wished he could agree with her, but he'd already been burned, and he knew better. Love didn't always last, no matter how well-intentioned the people were who stumbled into it. And he'd loved Vickie once upon a time.

"I'm jaded," he admitted.

Avery's gaze met his and then she nodded slowly. "I know..."

Was it so obvious? But standing with her in the starlit night, he wished he could forget about logic and ideals just for a little while, and let himself feel something again. But he knew what was waiting for him if he did—recriminations, hurt feelings, resentment when he had to tell yet another woman that he couldn't give her what she needed. Besides, if he started something up with an employee, he'd also find himself out of work.

She dropped her gaze and looked at her watch. "I have an early morning."

"Yeah, me, too."

Avery turned toward the bunkhouse, and he realized he didn't want her to go. She'd told him already that she was in town to learn more about her mother, but there was more to it—call it a gut feeling, but he was seldom wrong.

"Wait." He kept his voice low, and she turned back. "So I've told you about me. Don't you think I deserve just a little bit of truth from you?"

"What do you want to know?"

"Why are you really in Hope?" he asked.

She was silent for a few beats, and for a moment he thought she might not answer. Then she said, "My mom left Hope pregnant and never came back. I never knew my dad, but I'd like to get to know him, if I get the chance."

Her dad... Had she applied for the only job available to buy herself a little more time in town...or did she think *Mr. Harmon* was her father? He had questions, but she was turning away again.

"Good night, Hank," she called softly over her shoulder. "See you at breakfast."

He waited until she got inside before he headed back toward the road. He was cynical from a messy divorce and she was looking for a dad she'd never met. It was the reality check he needed. Attraction was one thing, but he liked to be realistic. He was her boss, and if he let those lines get blurred, he'd lose his job, smear his reputation and find himself back down at the bottom of the heap on another ranch. He had a cousin who owned about eight hundred acres, but he didn't want to work for Chet Granger. That felt too much like cap in hand. He wanted to build a career for himself that was based on his ability, not on a cousin's sense of duty. He'd worked too hard to get where he was on the Harmon ranch to ruin it with a flirtation, especially with someone who was here with ulterior motives.

He was a good cowboy, a better ranch manager and a bossy SOB who knew how to go it alone.

He'd stick to his strengths.

Chapter Six

The next morning's breakfast turned out rather well. She'd made scrambled eggs, pancakes, sausages, toast and porridge. Her timing was still off and she ended up serving the eggs cold, but no one complained, which at this point was Avery's goal. She didn't burn anything, either. When Hank had surveyed the breakfast spread, he'd shot her a grin and given her a thumbs-up. She'd never felt more accomplished in her life, and she felt a smile come to her lips now as she remembered it.

She wasn't supposed to be looking forward to seeing Hank, but last night had shown her a different side to the cowboy. Under that reserved, commanding exterior was a sweet guy. She could still remember the feeling of her hand in his, the sensation of his hand clamped against her side as the skunks investigated them. Except she was leaving in a week to reopen the flower shop, and there were rules around here that could ruin Hank's whole career. Entertaining these thoughts was a waste of time and energy.

She wrung out her dishcloth and hung it over the tap, then turned in time to see the swinging door open.

It wasn't Hank, it was Louis, his hat tucked under his arm, and she brightened. Her father had come to find her, instead of her pursuing him.

"Good morning, Mr. Harmon," she said.

"Good morning." The older man's cowboy boots echoed against the tiled floor as he walked into the kitchen and looked around. "How are you settling in?"

"Really well," she said. "I think breakfast was a success."

Louis nodded. "Yes, I think so."

Did that mean her job was still safe? It was strange to be wondering at the stability of a job she was about to quit, but keeping it for a week mattered. It was her chance to get to know Louis on some level. She might not ever call him Dad, but she'd never forgive herself if she squandered this time.

"I actually came by to give you these." Louis pulled an envelope out of his pocket. "I was going through some old photos last night, and I found these pictures of your mother from when we were both teenagers. I thought you might want them."

"Pictures?" Winona had never shown her any photos from her teenage years, and Avery eagerly accepted the envelope. "Thanks."

"I was thinking about your mom…" He smiled sadly. "I hadn't thought about her in a long time, and with your arrival, well…it brought back some memories."

Avery opened the envelope. She examined the first photo: four teenagers in the bed of a pickup truck. They were wearing a lot of denim, and she spotted her mother right away. Her hair was teased up in the front, the rest of it in permed curls. Like the others, she wore a faded jean jacket and she sat with her elbow resting on a boy's thigh who was looking at her adoringly. He wore a faded baseball cap backward. Could that be Louis in his youth?

"Who is that?" she asked, pointing to the enamored boy.

"Chris Mayfield," Louis replied. "Football player."

So, not her father. She flipped to the next photo, her mother sitting with some other teenage girls, all of them laughing at something. Her mother had a cigarette between her fingers and a bottle of beer between her boots. She had to look twice to make sure—this was not the mother she remembered!

"My mother smoked and drank?" Avery shook her head. "I'd never have thought…"

"She didn't tell you about that, huh?"

"Not a peep."

"I'm a father, and I've kept a few secrets of my own from my twins. As a parent, you want them to make positive choices, and you certainly don't want your youthful mistakes to serve as a bad example, you know."

"I suppose I'm old enough now to be left unscathed," she said wryly.

The next picture showed her mother standing alone beside that same pickup truck again. She wasn't posed. She was looking down at her fingernail, her lips pursed in concentration. Her hair shone in a halo of backlit sunlight, and there was something almost soulful in her mother's expression. This was the kind of snapshot a

young man took when he felt something for the subject—
the kind of beauty a guy on the sidelines would see.

"Who took this one?" Avery asked.

"Me." Louis's voice was low.

She looked closer at the photo. "Did you love her?"

Louis cleared his throat and glanced away. "Well,
you see…it was a long time ago."

"You must have had some sort of thing between
you…" she prompted.

"No." He shook his head. "I think I told you before.
We were friends, your mom and I. Good friends, even.
But she didn't go out with me. I was a bit of a dork back
then. Look—"

He tugged out the last photo, a snapshot of Winona
and Louis together. She had her arm through his, and
he was smiling. There were about six inches between
her hip and his. Louis was skinny, with some acne and
a cowlick in the front of his hair, and his expression in
the photo was one of doting admiration.

"You look like you had a bit of a crush," she said
with a low laugh.

"We all did," Louis replied. "Your mom was more
grown-up than the other girls. At least it seemed that
way to me. She was popular, too, but she wasn't interested in guys like me. I…well, I hadn't exactly bloomed
yet, so to speak."

"Hmm." Obviously, something had happened at
some point between them, and maybe Louis was too
much of a gentleman to say. Or too much of a coward.
She wasn't sure which.

"If you see that girl there—in the background,"

Louis said. Avery could just make out a girl standing some distance from the truck in the first photo. She was plump, with teased hair, and looked to be chewing her nail. "I married that one."

"That's your wife?" she asked in surprise.

"That's her. Carla. She hated your mom. I'm sorry—that's an awful thing to say, but since they're both in Heaven now, I imagine they'd be past all the pettiness. But Carla hated Winona because Winona was so…" He shook his head. "I don't know. Womanly. She didn't walk, she sashayed. And Carla was a country girl who lifted bales all summer. She was no dummy, either. She saw the way I looked at your mom, and ever after she couldn't stand her. I hadn't asked Carla out yet in that picture."

This version of her mother was so different from the Winona Southerly Avery had grown up with. Her mother had been fun, but cautious. She toed the line, didn't swear, watched the length of her hemlines. She was a church lady to the core…but obviously not *quite* to the core. Avery kind of liked that—the rebel in her youthful mother was appealing.

Her mother had *sashayed*.

"My mom was so careful not to even look like she was flirting… She volunteered in church, went to Bible study midweek…" And maybe this had been why her mother had been so cautious in everything—there didn't seem to be a lot of love lost for the sexy, teenage beauty.

"Chris Mayfield is the pastor at our church now," Louis said.

"This guy?" She held up the photo with her mother in the bed of the pickup.

"That's the one." Louis chuckled. "His parents sent him to Bible college straight after high school, and I guess it worked. He went on to a seminary, and he moved back about fifteen years ago as the local pastor."

"Was she dating Chris?" Avery asked. They certainly looked like a couple, except their relationship wasn't the one that produced her.

Louis nodded. "Off and on. She wasn't too serious about anyone in particular."

Was Louis trying to make a point here? Because it sounded to her like he was trying to steer her toward Chris Mayfield. She hadn't told Louis that she was looking for her father…but she had told Hank. At any rate, the good pastor wasn't her father, and she knew that.

And maybe her mother had been the reason that Chris's parents had promptly sent him away… A girl he used to date ended up pregnant, and they wanted to get him as far away from her as possible. While she knew that Chris wasn't her father, had the possibility occurred to his parents? Frankly, it sounded like a whole lot of judgment and cowardice to her, and she could see why her mother had left town to raise her daughter. Winona had done just fine on her own away from the drama and she'd been a good mother—strong, resolute, devoted. Young and single didn't add up to anything negative. She just got an earlier start than most, and considering that she'd passed away so young, maybe that was best. She'd been able to see her daughter grow into womanhood. Avery knew Winona had done an admirable job in raising her, and the thought of this town's judgment about her mother, even after all these years, rankled her.

"This girl here—" Louis tapped the photo of the girls laughing together "—she's now the principal of the high school."

"Really?" Avery looked up. "And she was friends with my mom?"

"Good friends." He nodded. "They had a falling out, though. I don't know what happened exactly. You know how kids are in high school."

"What's her name?" Avery asked.

"Hillary Neufeld." Louis said. "You said you wanted to know more about your mother, and the high school is a good place to start. You know your mom's cheer-leading days, I'm sure. There are pictures of her up in the hallway."

Cheerleading?

"I actually didn't know that…" How was it possible that her mom had lived this life and then never said a word about it? But talking with a woman who had known her mother might be a nice balance from what she'd heard from Louis. Louis was holding firm on the story that he and her mother had been nothing but friends. Perhaps Hillary would have a different perspec-tive on Winona's relationship with Louis.

"Thank you," she said. "I think I will check it out."

"Well…" Louis nodded and gave her a smile. "I'll leave you to it, then. Hank is going into town today for some errands. He could probably give you a lift."

"Do you think he'd mind?" she asked.

"Don't see why. I'll tell him to come find you. He normally heads out by ten."

"Thanks."

Louis left and Avery stood for several beats in the middle of the kitchen, her mind spinning. Her mother had a life filled with friends, boyfriends, cheerleading... and then ran away from it all so effectively that Avery had no idea about any of it. If she hadn't seen the photo evidence, she'd never have believed it.

And yet Louis stayed adamant about his friend-zoned status with her mother. Why? Was it her? Or was he doing the exact same thing her mother had done, hanging on to a version of the past that he figured his youngest kids needed?

HANK PULLED HIS cell phone out of his shirt pocket and looked down at the text. It was from his boss.

Hank, I'm assuming you're still going into town this morning. I told the cook you'd be leaving at about 10. Take her with you, if you could. Thanks.

The cook. Funny how Hank had stopped thinking of her as "the cook," and she'd become something more. He didn't like that... If Avery were just a little less interesting, less attractive...less *her*, he'd be able to see her as the employee she was and wouldn't give her another thought between times. But as it was, he'd been beating himself up for last night's familiarity. That was well past professional courtesy, and Mr. Harmon didn't fool around with his rules. If one person could get away with breaking them—especially the ranch manager—then everyone gave it a try.

It *had* been dark, and holding her hand *had* been the easiest way to guide her down the road without twisting an ankle or getting sprayed by a skunk, but it hadn't done a whole lot for keeping those boss-employee boundaries neatly drawn. He might have kissed her last night if he'd had less self-control. Standing there in the moonlight with her, those big green eyes fixed on him, had felt like the most natural thing in the world, but someone would have seen him, and he'd be fired as an example. Still…he found himself wondering what it might feel like to tug her closer, brush the hair away from her face and catch those soft, pink lips with his—

He pulled his mind away from the edge. This could ruin everything he'd worked for over the years. Mr. Harmon thought Hank was trustworthy, and once trust was lost…

But Mr. Harmon was more than a boss, too. When Vickie left Hank, Mr. Harmon had taken him aside and treated him more like a friend or a son, and helped him to move on. In return, when Mrs. Harmon died in the riding accident, Hank had been there for his boss. He knew heartbreak, and for some reason, Mr. Harmon had been able to accept Hank's support easier than someone else's. That kind of bond, forged in the trenches, as it were, mattered more than a simple boss-employee relationship, and to lose Mr. Harmon's trust wasn't even an option.

As he drove down the dirt road that led away from the barns and went toward the bunkhouse, he had to wonder what his boss thought of Avery. Hank's interest should be obvious—she was gorgeous, and he was a red-blooded male. But Mr. Harmon couldn't be falling for her, could he? At his age? Calling her "the cook" didn't exactly undo the unusual request that Hank bring her along on his weekly trip to town. Mr. Harmon was taking an interest in Avery, too. But last night Avery had told him that she was here looking for her father...

Could Louis be the father she was hoping to get to know?

He pushed that suspicion back. Jumping to conclusions was never a good idea, especially when his boss's reputation might be at stake. Hank was a loyal guy, and he owed his boss a whole lot. He hadn't climbed to this position without learning some hard-won wisdom along the way, like never assume anything without some pretty solid proof.

Hank pulled up in front of the bunkhouse and he didn't even have to turn off the motor because Avery was waiting by the door. She wore a pair of blue jeans and a white blouse. Her hair hung fiery and loose around her shoulders, and when she saw him, she shot him a smile. Smiles like that one made keeping those boundaries all the harder.

"Good morning," she said as she hopped up into the cab next to him. She banged the door shut and reached for her seat belt. The scent of vanilla wafted through the cab. He put the truck into gear and headed back to the road.

"Thanks for bringing me along," she said. "As long as I'm back by one, I'll have enough time to cook dinner."

"Meat loaf tonight?" he asked.

"In all its glory. This is one I know how to make."

She had started to settle in, and it was good to see. As a manager, he'd done a good job getting her self-sufficient in her position. He hadn't had to help her out in the kitchen for a full day now, and he wasn't supposed to be wishing that she'd need more help from him…but he was—just a little bit.

"So where are you wanting to go in town?" he asked.

"The high school, actually," she replied. "Mr. Harmon says that there are pictures of my mom from her cheerleading days on the walls, and the principal there was one of her friends."

Small world. Actually, it was just a small town, but her mother had been friends with Hillary?

"Hillary Neufeld is my cousin," he said.

"Seriously?" She shot him a look of surprise.

"Yeah. I can give you an introduction, if you want."

"That would be great," she said. "That's lucky."

"In a town this size, there are a lot of family connections," he said with a short laugh. "The Grangers are a big ranching family out here. My dad didn't inherit any land, though. Mr. Harmon is my ex-wife's second cousin. That's a fun one for you."

"Wow…" She turned toward him. "So, when you got divorced, that didn't make things awkward for you at work?"

"Nah." Should he talk about this? But he couldn't help himself. She was easy to talk to, and somehow it felt good just to open up for a change. "I think Mr. Harmon felt a bit sorry for me. Vickie wasn't a bad person, but we wanted really different things out of life. When

I took the job on the Harmon ranch, she hated it, and I couldn't do too much about that. I mean, I needed to support her, and I made more as ranch manager here than as a hand somewhere else. She liked the money, she just hated being stuck out here."

"And Mr. Harmon could see that you'd done your best," she concluded.

"Yeah, pretty much." Blood was only so thick, and Vickie had embarrassed Mr. Harmon, too.

Hank drove past the main house and waved at Owen, who was working under the hood of his truck in the driveway. Owen was a good kid—a man, just about. There'd been a time when he would watch Hank working on the ranch vehicles, and now he was tinkering away on his own Ford. Hank was proud.

"So…you'd say that Mr. Harmon was fair," she said.

"Definitely." He braked at the main road that lead toward Hope and let another pickup pass before he made his turn.

"Is he the kind of man who lies?" she asked.

That was a strange question, especially about the boss. Mr. Harmon was moral to a fault.

"Where is this coming from? Louis Harmon is a straight shooter. If he's told you something, you can trust it."

Hank glanced over at her and she was looking out the window, her face turned from him.

"You said last night that you were hoping to meet your dad," he said. "Is your question…connected?"

It seemed that Louis had known her mother years ago, but did he know who Avery's father was, too? A lot happened in this town, and if a man was wise, he kept his mouth shut. Still, gossip was the fuel for Hope, Montana…

"It is…" She looked over at him, green eyes filled with misgiving. "Hank, this is really delicate. I…" She sighed. "Can I trust you to be discreet?"

Those eyes weren't appealing to her boss, they were appealing to the man in him. And blast it, that was the part of him that always seemed to respond to her.

"Yeah, of course," he replied.

"Louis Harmon is my father." Her gaze flickered toward him, and she licked her lips, waiting.

It took a moment for those words to sink in, then he shot her an incredulous look. "What?"

"My mom never wanted to tell me who my father was. I asked over and over again, but she always said it didn't matter. And I suppose it didn't. He never contributed anything to my childhood. It was always just Mom and me. On her deathbed, I asked again, and this time she gave me a name—Louis Harmon."

Hank let out a long breath. "Wait… So does he know about this?"

"I'm not entirely sure." She leaned her head back against the headrest. "I haven't told him, at least. I'm still trying to figure out if my mother told him at some point and he just wasn't interested in the role."

"If he thought you were his daughter—" Hank began.

"He might not want his younger kids to know," she interrupted. "That's why I wanted your opinion of how honest he is. But then again, this isn't an ordinary situation, is it?"

"So why haven't you said anything yet?" Hank asked. This seemed like the kind of thing that wouldn't get easier the more time passed.

"I was going to," she confessed. "But it's harder than you think to announce something like that."

"I could see that…" He took off his hat and dropped it into his lap, then ran a hand over his hair. "So you applied for this job—"

"To get to know my father," she confirmed.

His gut had been right, he realized. She'd had some ulterior motives, just not the ones he'd imagined. This was a whole lot worse than a gold-digging beauty. This would be personal for Louis—really personal. And the twins…yeah, they wouldn't take this easily, either.

"When Louis hired you, it was because we needed a cook," he said. "This isn't a game, you know."

"And I haven't treated it like one!" she countered. "Granted there was more to the story, but I offered to step down and you told me not to. Remember?"

Yeah, vaguely. They didn't have anyone else applying right now anyway, but he couldn't help but feel a little bit duped.

"You must have talked to Mr. Harmon some," Hank said, trying to pull it all together in his head. "I mean, he did get me to drive you into town…"

"I've asked questions about my mom, that's all." She sighed. "He's pointing me in the direction of the pastor at the church here in town."

"Pastor Mayfield?" Hank knew him quite well. He was married with two daughters. A nice family. Pastor

Mayfield was a good preacher, too. "So, he knew your mom back then?"

"He dated my mom, actually," she replied. "And it seems to me that Louis is suggesting that Chris might be my father."

Mr. Harmon obviously didn't know what was coming at him right now, and he probably thought he was helping by giving Avery some clues into her mother's past. But if his boss had been intimate with Avery's mom, then he should be able to connect the dots himself… right? So knowing Mr. Harmon like he did—

"Is it possible that Chris *is* your dad?" Hank asked.

"My mom would know who my father was, don't you think?" she asked drily. "She gave me his name. She wouldn't have done that if it weren't true. You didn't know my mother."

Hank shrugged. She was right—he hadn't known her. But he did know Mr. Harmon, and he wasn't the kind of man to send his daughter off on a wild-goose chase to save face. He'd do the right thing. So either Chris Mayfield was an actual contender in her paternity, or Louis had no idea he was her father.

"Well…" Hank said carefully. "I've known Mr. Harmon a long time, and we've been through a lot. He isn't the kind of man who would lie about something like this. If he thought he was your father, he'd face it head-on. I can guarantee you that."

"Okay." She sucked in a breath and nodded. "Good to know."

"Do you mind if I ask what your plan is?" he asked.

"I don't really know..." She sighed. "But if you could, please keep this private for now."

"For how long?" he asked. "Because I owe Louis a lot, and I'm not really comfortable keeping this kind of secret."

"I can understand that," she said, fixing her deep, soulful eyes on him. "But if you could just give me a few days. I don't have much longer that I can even stay here in Hope, anyway. I have to get back to the flower shop. So let's say three days."

That wasn't an outrageous request, and he wasn't promising to keep his mouth shut for longer than that. Louis had always been straight with him, but this wasn't Hank's secret, either. He didn't really belong in the middle of this mess.

"Okay," he agreed. "Three days, but you've got to tell him the truth, Avery. He deserves to know."

And what would happen then, he had no idea, but at least Louis would have the chance to deal with it directly. And Avery... He looked over and saw her chewing the side of her cheek. She'd be on her way anyway—out of town and back to Kansas.

It finally all made sense. That nagging in the back of his mind was stilled. For all those irritating suspicions, he wished he hadn't been right after all, and that she was just a woman wanting to work as a cook on a ranch...nothing more complicated. Then the biggest problem he'd have was his attraction to her...because even knowing everything that he did right now, the way he felt about her hadn't changed. And that was dangerous ground.

Chapter Seven

After a trip to the ranch supply store, where Avery watched as Hank picked up some mousetraps, salt licks and several large bags of ear tags, Hank drove them over to the high school. It was a low brick building that was looking a little faded. The bike rack out front was full, and from some open windows, Avery could hear the drone of voices. School was still in session, even if the weather felt like full summer.

So this was her mother's high school. It felt strange to be looking at the place where her mother had been pregnant with her. Winona had told Avery a little bit of the story—how she'd been about five months pregnant by graduation, and she'd tried to hide her baby bump under the grad gown. But everyone knew by then, anyway. Winona had graduated, and a week later, she moved to Kansas, where an aunt helped her to get ready for the birth of her baby.

Her classmates hadn't been cruel, exactly. Winona said that she'd needed a fresh start—her reputation wasn't going to improve any if she stayed in Hope. Avery wondered what it would be like to walk the hallways of this school five months pregnant. The whispers. The gossip. The curiosity over the father...

It had been a long time since Avery had been in a high school, herself, and the couple of kids she saw wandering out of the there looked so young. She'd felt so much older when she'd been a senior in high school, but she'd probably been just as fresh faced.

"So your mom was a cheerleader?" Hank said as they trotted up the front steps.

"Apparently," she replied.

"What about you?" Hank asked. "Pompoms? Short little skirt?"

Avery laughed and shook her head. That couldn't have been further from her own high school experience. "Debate club and school newspaper."

Her mother had been quite judgmental about cheerleading and the jocks who played on the sports teams. Avery was starting to wonder what her mother had been through. Maybe those five months of pregnancy while she still attended school had been more traumatizing than she'd admitted to. Still, Avery hadn't been the cheerleading type. She'd liked to read. And debate—she'd been rather skilled in that arena.

"Seriously?" Hank looked her over. "Okay, maybe I see it."

Hank pulled open the door for her and let her pass through first. His boots clunked against the linoleum floor behind her as he followed her inside. There was no air-conditioning in this old building, and it smelled like gym shoes and orange peels. The unseasonal June heat seemed to make it worse.

"This way," he said, his fingers lingering on the back of her arm before leading her toward the office. The touch was casual—polite even—but there was something about his gentlemanly gestures that sparked some warm feelings in her, and she quickly tried to tamp them down.

There were a few cabinets of trophies along the walls, some signs posted about graduation fees and a large glossy poster about the dangers of smoking. The office was located a few yards away from the front doors, windows open into the hallway.

"Good morning," Hank said to the secretary with a smile. "Wondering if Mrs. Neufeld has some time to chat with us."

"Are you parents?" Her gaze flickered to Avery questioningly. She obviously thought Avery looked too young to have a child in high school.

"I'm Hillary's cousin," Hank said. "And this is Avery Southerly. We're just sleuthing out some family history and Hillary might be of help."

"Oh... Well, I'm sure you could ask her." The phone rang. "Feel free to wait," the secretary said with a distracted smile. "She'll be back soon." She picked up the receiver and turned away.

Avery could hear a woman's amplified voice filtering down the hallways. "...at which point you will receive your diploma. The teacher who hands it to you will say a few words to you. A photographer will take your picture then—so don't rush, but also be respectful of the graduates coming behind you..."

"Thanks," Avery said. "We'll just be out there."

The secretary nodded, and they went out into the hallway again. One stretch of hallway was lined by lockers, and above them were framed graduating class photos going back through the years. Avery looked down that hallway. It was possible she'd find her mother's photo on that wall.

"So what about me screams debate club to you?" she asked, glancing up at him.

Hank's slow, controlled gaze moved over at her, then he said, "I don't know…you look wholesome."

"Debate club could get pretty feisty, you know," she countered.

"Alright," he said, a teasing smile tugging at his lips. "Feisty and wholesome."

Well, maybe she was. But while her high school years were less exciting than her mother's seemed to have been, she'd had good friends and no regrets. But she wasn't the one who'd gone to school here. This was also Hank's old school, wasn't it?

"What about you?" she asked. "4-H? Future Farmers of America?"

"Football." He raised an eyebrow. "And I was pretty good, too."

Avery grinned. "Really?"

Somehow, it was hard to imagine this serious cowboy in football gear, but then she'd never imagined her mom as a cheerleader, either.

"And 4-H," he conceded with a small smile. "I was complicated."

That was one way to describe him. She still hadn't figured him out. He was strong and tough, but there was a tender core that he protected. Because of his divorce? Or was it more than that? She wished she knew.

"You still seem complicated," she confessed.

"It's all a big act," he replied. "I'm actually very simple. All work and no fun."

"I don't think so." She turned toward him and looked up into his face. "Last night when you walked me back—"

"I don't really want to talk about that." He glanced away. Was that embarrassment she sensed from him?

"—you opened up," she went on, ignoring his protest. "I saw it. You looked me in the eye and you weren't the boss anymore. You were…a really sweet guy who cared."

He'd held her hand until the moon came out, and then he'd moved that strand of hair away from her lips… Maybe she was reading more into the moment, but she'd wondered if he was thinking about kissing her. It was the way his gaze had lingered on her mouth. He hadn't been the bossy ranch manager out there in the moonlight.

"Was I?" He sighed. "That was an accident."

"Maybe so," she agreed. "But I still saw it. There is a whole lot more to you that you keep hidden all the time. It must be hard work."

"What's hard work?" he asked. The smile was gone; he met her gaze for a silent beat.

"All that hiding."

"I'm careful not to give the wrong impression," he replied. "I'm not a guy who toys with women."

"What, hiding that you might actually be fun?" she asked with a teasing smile.

"That I'm available."

His words made the smile on her lips evaporate. Was that what he was worried about, that she'd fall for him like some young innocent? Maybe she should be a little more careful, too, about the impression she gave. She knew what was good for her, and she knew what she wanted out of life. She wasn't about to do something so stupid as to fall for an emotionally unavailable cowboy from her mother's hometown in another state. Her life—and her future—lay in Kansas. She was only here to introduce herself to her father, and she hadn't lost sight of that.

"Don't flatter yourself, cowboy," she said with a small smile. "I've got a flower shop in Kansas that I'm going back to."

"I didn't mean—" He winced.

"Yes, you did," she replied. "And it's alright. We're on the same page. You can relax."

He took a breath and opened his mouth as if he were going to say something, then he turned back to the photos on the wall. "That's my class there."

He nodded up at a picture and she watched Hank as he looked at the faces. His classmates—the people who had grown up with him, known him since he was a kid. Maybe he would hold himself back less with them. He had to have someone who understood him, made him feel less alone. Avery scanned the young faces, wondering if she could pick him out.

"Fourth from the left, third row," he said.

Her eyes moved to the appropriate photo, and she couldn't help but grin. There he was—all young and innocent. He was a good-looking guy, and she could see how the years had changed him. He was tougher now, stronger.

"You look like you were a sweet kid," she said.

"I thought I was quite manly at that point." He laughed softly. She looked closer at the photo and then back at Hank. The years had solidified him, hardened him into real manhood.

"I was six months away from getting engaged in that picture," he went on. "I had all these plans for the future… I wanted kids back then. I figured by the time I was this age, I'd have at least four sons. Maybe even my own ranch."

"What if you had girls?" she asked.

"As long as they could ride and rope, I'd have been happy." The smile slipped from his face. "Well, life didn't work out that way, and maybe I was too stubborn to be much good at it, anyway. Turned out I wasn't much of a husband, either. But back then—" he nodded toward the picture "—I was oblivious to all that."

"You're ranch manager now," she said. "I'd call that success."

"I've definitely worked for it," he said, but there was something in his tone that suggested he didn't have it all yet. What was missing from his version of success? she wondered. Was it his wife—the woman who'd walked away from him? To have chosen some other guy over this brooding, handsome cowboy… Avery wasn't sure how a woman could do that. But this wasn't the time or the place to be thinking those things. Hank had said so himself—he wasn't available. And she wasn't sticking around, either, so…

"I wonder where my mom's picture is." They were near the end of the hallway, and it looked like they didn't have class photos going back more than twenty years.

Behind them in the gym, a woman's voice had been replaced by a man's, talking about "…showboating on the platform." Some things never changed—like warning teenage boys not to moon friends and family. The gym door opened and a woman in a navy suit who looked about her mother's age came out of the gymnasium.

"That's Hillary," Hank said, and he waved.

A smile came to Mrs. Neufeld's face and she headed in their direction, pumps echoing through the hallway. The private camaraderie of the moment evaporated as her mother's friend strode toward them. Maybe Avery would get some answers.

HANK GLANCED AROUND Hillary's office. He'd been a generally good kid when he was in high school. He wasn't a real studier, but he passed all his classes, which was a prerequisite for playing football. And he'd liked football—more than math or English. He'd also liked riding and being out on the open range, breathing in the scent of grass and scrub. But football satisfied that part of him that liked a goal, points, a clear victory. It also gave him a chance at college, and he wanted to study agriculture most of all.

He'd sat in this very office while his principal gave him the good news that he was being offered a football scholarship to Montana State. He would have been thrilled—this had been the goal all along. That football scholarship would have made college possible, but senior year, his situation changed, and he couldn't put off working for the four years it would take to get a degree. He needed money now—he needed a job.

Hank could still remember the look of disappointment on the principal's face. And education was a future, but Hank wasn't willing to explain. It was personal, and he had made his choice. Standing by a decision was a mark of manhood. Like standing by a woman he never should have married… Had that been a mark of character or stupidity?

"What can I do for you today?" Hillary looked a lot like the Granger side of the family. She was tall, slim and had a wide, toothy smile. She'd gone to college—two degrees, actually—and she'd made the family proud.

Hank made the introductions and they all took a seat.

"I was told that you knew my mother," Avery said, jumping right in. "Winona Southerly. Do you remember her?"

"Winona?" Hillary's eyebrows shot up. "Yes, of course. That was a long time ago, though. I knew her when we were attending this very high school."

"Yes, that's what I heard," Avery confirmed.

"Are you…" Hillary paused. "When she left, she was—" She stopped again. Yeah, Hank could see the awkwardness of that question.

"Yes, I'm the one she was pregnant with senior year," Avery confirmed.

His cousin breathed out a long breath and nodded. "I'm glad to meet you, Avery. How is your mother doing?"

"She passed away a couple of months ago," Avery replied. "Breast cancer."

Silence stretched for a couple of beats, then Hillary blinked a few times and said, "I'm so sorry… I hadn't heard. My condolences."

Hank wondered if he should have quietly excused himself before they started talking. If he left now, he'd just be interrupting them, so he sat there, mildly uncomfortable.

"The thing is, my mom never talked about Hope and the life she had before she moved to Kansas, and since she passed away I wanted to find out what I could, what kind of person she was back then, that sort of thing."

"I'm not sure what I can tell you," Hillary said slowly.

"You were friends, though," Avery pressed. "What was she like?"

That seemed like a fair question to Hank. Who didn't wonder what their parents were like before parenthood?

Hillary smiled sadly. "She was very popular. I wasn't. You know how those things can be."

"Is it true you had a falling out with her?"

Hillary nodded. "My boyfriend preferred her to me. I was upset about that, and Winona dated him for a while. She and I never did patch it up. I'm sorry about that now."

That was a gentle way of putting it, Hank noted. Winona had stolen her boyfriend?

"Who were you dating?" Avery asked. "Do you mind if I ask that?"

"Oh, not at all." Hillary shook her head. "It was ages ago. He was a young man named Philip Vernon."

"He's a mechanic here in town," Hank offered.

"Ah." Avery smiled wanly. "Okay… Thanks."

"I've got an old yearbook from the year we graduated." Hillary spun her chair around and went over to a bookshelf on the far wall. She pulled a hardcover book from the bottom shelf and brought it back to the desk. She flipped through the first few pages, then handed it over, open to a page of candid shots.

"That's your mother there—" She pointed. "And there…"

Hank looked over Avery's shoulder to see where Hillary pointed. He could see a fine-featured girl who looked an awful lot like Avery, except she was blonde where Avery was fiery red. There was a photo of her sitting next to Chris Mayfield in her cheerleading uniform, an easy smile on her face. Some things didn't change over the years, and one of them was cheerleaders. No matter what year, you put a cute girl in that little uniform, and the guys would follow her around like puppies.

Vickie had been a cheerleader, too—cute and perky, full of offbeat humor. He'd liked the way she bounced around and cheered for the team, and one day after practice, he'd asked her out. Dating a cheerleader was a status thing for the guys, but he and Vickie hadn't really been a good match. The only thing they had in common was football.

"Who's that?" Avery asked, and Hank tuned back into the conversation.

"That would be—" Hillary turned the yearbook around and squinted at the photo "—Ned Pine, I believe."

"A friend?" Avery asked, and he caught the nervousness in her voice.

"Well…" Hillary's expression froze. "I'm not sure what you're wanting me to say here."

"I want to know if he was a friend, or something more." Avery's tone grew terse, but she was clutching her hands together in a white-knuckled grip. She was nervous.

"I…" Hillary sighed. "I honestly don't know. Winona was—" She looked at Hank helplessly, and Hank just stared back. He didn't know anything about Hillary's old high school friend. He couldn't help her out here. The only thing he could identify with was what it was like to have a pregnant girlfriend in senior year.

"Okay," Avery said with a sigh. "What about Louis Harmon?"

That caught Hank's attention. That was a good question—one he was curious about, too. Was Mr. Harmon one of the guys Winona had been involved with, or was he in the clear?

"Avery," Hillary said softly. "Are you looking for your father?"

"I suppose that's a bit obvious, isn't it?" Avery sighed. "Yes. I'm not interested in forcing anything… I'm not asking for money or anything like that. I just…with mom's passing…" Tears welled in her eyes, and Hank leaned toward her. He'd have put an arm around her if he thought it would comfort her, but that didn't seem right in this situation.

"I understand," Hillary said softly. "The thing is,

Avery, your mom had quite a few boyfriends over senior year. She was involved with a lot of guys."

Avery stiffened, licked her lips.

"I don't say this to speak ill of your mom," Hillary
went on gently, "but if you're looking for your dad, it
might be difficult."

"And Louis?" Avery asked woodenly.

"He was a friend of hers. I don't know how involved
they were, but…I suppose it's possible."

Hank hadn't wanted to hear that…for his boss's sake.
But if Mr. Harmon were Avery's father, he needed to
know that, too. A man took care of his responsibilities.

Chapter Eight

Avery watched as the telephone poles crept past her window, the lines looping lazily. They were on their way back to the ranch, but the earlier cheeriness had slipped away. Thinking back on it, she should have done that visit with Hillary Neufeld with more privacy. She hadn't expected to find out that Louis had been right about her mother—looking for love in all the wrong places. He wasn't the only one to have that opinion about Winona.

Stealing her friend's boyfriend, selfish behavior... Winona hadn't been that kind of woman. She'd been moral to a fault, very black-and-white about things. She'd refused to let Avery date until she was seventeen, and then before the boy picked her up, her mother had given her a few self-defense lessons. Her mother had told her in all earnestness, *You have no right getting into a car with a boy unless you know how to maim him from the passenger seat.*

The rules for dating had been lengthy and written in stone. She'd hated that. Avery wasn't going to make her mother's mistake—her mother had drilled that into her from the beginning. So Avery thought she deserved a little more trust in her ability to make good choices. Winona disagreed.

Avery was to be back exactly thirty minutes after the movie ended. She was permitted to sit and talk with the boy in her own living room, with her mother close enough by to pop in at inopportune moments. Avery was raised with the ideal of abstinence until marriage, *because you don't want to be a teen mother like I was, dear. It's harder than it needs to be. You want a husband by your side. Trust me on that.*

Winona knew the dangers from experience, and she wanted something different for her daughter, but Avery had always had the distinct impression that her mother's pregnancy had been a shocking one-off accident. She'd heard stories about girls who had sex once and discovered they were pregnant, and she'd assumed that her mother was the same—a living, breathing morality tale. She now felt a little foolish about that. Wasn't that the joke, that kids always thought their parents had had sex only enough times to conceive them, and never again?

"I'm sorry to have dragged you into that," Avery said, breaking the lengthy silence. She turned back toward him.

"It's okay." He glanced at her, then back to the road. "That wasn't easy to hear, I'll bet."

"No." She swallowed hard. "I almost wish I'd left well enough alone. She didn't want me to know this stuff."

"Does it change anything?" Hank asked. "Times

have changed. It isn't quite as shocking as it was twenty-five years ago."

"I know…" She sighed. "But you didn't know my mom. Having me find this out—it would have really embarrassed her. She worked hard to hide all of this from me."

It had embarrassed Avery, too. She'd expected to discover that her mother had been quiet and nerdy. She thought that her mom might have been the kind of girl who kept to herself and didn't have many friends, who fell in love with a boy and things went too quickly… She'd pieced together the crumbs of information her mother had let fall, and she could imagine her mother heartbroken at a breakup, determined to start fresh alone. But now she saw that that hadn't been the case. Her mother had been outgoing and flirtatious. She'd had a lot of boyfriends. She'd crossed lines and betrayed friendships.

But still, she couldn't imagine that her mother would have lied about who her father was…especially not knowing that she didn't have much longer for this world. Winona had truly and deeply believed that she was going to meet her Maker, and she wouldn't have had a lie stand between her and God…not then.

"It's hard having people remember my mother that way," Avery said quietly. "Because I remember her much differently. They didn't know her like I did."

The people of Hope didn't know her like the people of Salina knew her, either. In Salina, she had a lot of friends. She'd been there for the baptisms of their babies, for their weddings and funerals. If they'd known the truth about Winona's past, would it have made a difference? Would they have trusted her like they did?

"Maybe my cousin was just jealous of her," Hank suggested. "She did say that her boyfriend preferred your mother. That might have colored her memory somewhat."

"Louis said the same thing," she confessed. "Without quite so many details, but he said that she'd been looking for love in all the wrong places here in Hope, and he was glad that she'd found the right places in Kansas."

Hank was silent.

"It might not be good news that Louis has another daughter," she said. "I was prepared for him to think that. I just wasn't prepared to agree with him."

Hank slowed and signaled a turn onto a side road. The tires crunched over gravel as he made the turn, and her gaze slid over the reeds growing in the marshy ditches. It looked like Kansas here—but Louis's joke had been more accurate than she'd ever imagined. She most certainly wasn't in Kansas anymore, and she ardently wished that she'd been content enough to just stay home.

"What do you mean, you agree with him?" Hank asked with a frown.

"I mean, with my mother's reputation, he might not be very proud for people to know that he'd been one of the guys she'd been with..." It felt horrible to say, but there had been a reason why her mother had never brought her back here. Her mother had a reputation, and Winona hadn't ever wanted to face it again.

"I think you're underestimating Mr. Harmon," Hank

replied, his voice low. "He'd want to know his daughter, no matter how you were conceived."

"You can't know that," she said. "I came here to tell him who I was, but that might have been a mistake."

"So what are you going to do?" Hank asked.

"I might go back, let this rest." She sighed. "It doesn't change how I see my mother. I just understand her a little better now. But it does change my expectations about my father."

Hank pushed his hat back and sighed. "A decent man wants to know, Avery."

"I might be doing him a favor," she replied. "What do I want from him at this point? To announce his secret to his teenage children? He's raising kids. That changes things."

"He will want to know." His voice grew firmer. "I know that."

"What makes you so sure?" she asked wryly. "Sometimes ignorance is bliss."

Her own ignorance felt like bliss right about now... She'd preferred the uninformed version of her mother's history—the nearly immaculate conception. It was more comfortable, and she knew for a fact that her mother preferred it, too.

"Because I've been there," Hank said.

Silence settled into the cab, the only sounds the motor and the whistle of air coming through the cracked-open window. Avery stared at Hank in surprise.

"What do you mean, you've been there?" she asked.

"Vickie was pregnant."

She frowned. "I didn't realize you had any children. I thought you said—"

"I don't. She got pregnant senior year, just like your mom. I'd gotten a football scholarship that was going to pay my way through a degree in agriculture. But with Vickie pregnant, I needed a job right away to provide for her, so I turned it down and went straight to work at the Mason ranch. I did the right thing and asked her to marry me. She miscarried before we got married, and I had a choice—walk away from her or stand by my word. Thing is, marriage is supposed to be for the good times and the bad, and losing the baby—that was the worst. So I decided that the right thing to do was to marry her. I'd proposed, and I'd been more than willing to get married when I thought we were having a baby, so that had to mean something."

"But you knew about her pregnancy," Avery said. "It's different."

"Yeah, but finding out that you've made a baby with someone changes things," he countered. "It did for me."

"What if she'd left town and you'd met someone else—someone you really loved deeply—and you started a family and built a life…and then that child came back?" she asked.

"She'd still be mine, Avery." His voice was low and warm, and his words sank deep into her heart. That was what a daughter longed to hear—that she belonged by virtue of her DNA. But they weren't talking about Hank, they were talking about Louis. Hank had a failed marriage under his belt, and Louis had had two decades of love with a wife he had adored.

"Thing is," Hank went on. "I never met my daughter. I was at football practice when Vickie was rushed to the hospital, and no one called me until it was over. I guess it all happened pretty quickly."

"That's awful." She winced. The father should have mattered just a little bit more.

"So I never saw her," Hank said. "But I loved her. And I still do. There's this little part of my heart that will always belong to the daughter I never met. A man deserves to hear the truth, Avery. And knowing my boss like I do, he's going to care."

"So you think I should stick to the original plan," she said slowly. "Let him know…"

"I can't tell you what to do," he said. "This is too personal for me to even pretend I can give you answers. But don't be scared away."

Avery was scared, she had to admit. She was scared of the rejection—seeing her father's face when he realized this terrible cook he'd employed was more than just a subpar worker, she was a twenty-four-year-old reminder of something he might not be terribly proud of…but then, the way Avery had imagined her conception—the one ill-conceived night that they both lived to regret—might not have been so far off the mark.

Louis said they were nothing more than friends, and it looked like Winona dated football players, not Future Farmers of America. So whatever happened between them, be it a pity connection Winona bestowed upon him or a brief entanglement, it might very well have been just once. Of all the possibilities, she didn't really want that one to be true. She'd wanted to find a father who had loved her mother. She'd wanted to find a man whose heart would have filled at the memory of the girl who got away. But that wasn't the truth.

Hank slowed the truck again, this time at the arch that read Harmon Ranch. They were back, and Avery had a decision. She could see this through and tell Louis what she knew, or she could do them all a favor and quit. They needed a real cook, not a stand-in who didn't have the guts to say why she was really here. She'd have to make her choice.

AFTER HANK DROPPED Avery at the canteen, he headed toward the barn. He had supplies to unload, but more than that, he needed time to sort through his thoughts.

He'd been married to Vickie longer than he'd been divorced, and talking with Avery had brought her back to mind as sharp as broken glass. When she'd walked out, it had broken his heart, but the betrayal was all the deeper because of what he'd given up for her. Because of her, he'd passed on a college scholarship. Because of the baby on the way, he'd proposed, and he'd stood by her during the upheavals of the miscarriage and the grief that followed. He could have walked away then— a lot of guys would have—but he hadn't. Tough times weren't an excuse to bail, so he'd followed through with his promise to marry her. A man was nothing if he wasn't good for his word. But what about a woman? She'd vowed love and fidelity, too.

Marriage wasn't what either of them expected, but Hank had been raised by two parents who loved each other dearly and who put every ounce of effort they could into maintaining their relationship. They put each other first, always. Hank had thought that if he just worked hard enough like his parents had, that he'd eventually reap a happy, devoted marriage, too. Except it hadn't worked that way for him and Vickie. No matter how hard he tried to make her happy, she only got more frustrated. And no matter how hard she tried to "loosen him up," he just couldn't do it. It went against his nature.

But still—he'd stood by her, and he'd believed she'd do the same for him. So when she left, he'd been even more deeply betrayed. After all, he could have walked away long before that and made it much easier on himself. He'd believed their vows were for a reason—because life together wasn't easier than life apart—not always.

Maybe it was for the best that they hadn't had any children. It seemed like a karmic punishment that their first child should be conceived accidentally, but once they'd gotten married and established the home that should have given future children a stable environment, they hadn't been able to conceive again. And they'd both wanted children even more than they'd wanted each other.

Which was why not having children when she finally walked out on him was probably for the best. The last thing they needed was to be fighting about custody or child support. No kid needed to be in the middle of that... But when their marriage ended, he'd vowed that he'd never just blindly do "the right thing" again. Good intentions and integrity of granite didn't guarantee happiness or even a fighting chance, and he'd learned that the hardest way possible.

That was also why he held back when it came to women now. He hadn't been enough for his wife. The thought of marriage left him feeling slightly panicked when he considered doing it again. So he figured he'd save any woman he got involved with the heartbreak and just be up front about where he stood.

The truck bumped over a pothole, the shocks squeaking with the force of the jolt. He muttered an oath under his breath and pulled his attention back to the road. The barn's round roof came into view, its red paint starting to crack and peel. It was definitely due for another coat. This was where they housed the cows that were recovering from illness or injury. Cattle that were given any medication had to be kept separate from the herd until it was out of their systems. Any meat that was tested in the slaughterhouse and came up positive for antibiotics would be at their expense, so they took this very seriously. No rancher wanted to take a financial hit like that.

Hank parked out front and hopped out of his truck. He grabbed the plastic bags of supplies and headed for the side door. It opened just as he got to it, and Owen came out. His hair was a mess of dark curls and he looked up at Hank gloomily.

"Hey, Uncle Hank. Need a hand?"

"Sure. Thanks." Hank passed Owen the bags of salt licks and they went into the barn together. "You okay, kid?"

"Yup."

That was a lie. Owen was ordinarily a pretty open, happy teen. This morose act was new.

"Put the salt licks in the cupboard," Hank said, and Owen did as he told him. "So what's going on?"

"Nothing."

"Look, Owen, I know you better than that," Hank said. "So what's her name?"

Owen smiled wanly. "Chloe."

"There you go. What's the problem?"

Owen regarded him in silence for a moment. "You'll tell my dad."

"No, I won't," Hank replied. "Unless it's something really weird…"

If his daughter had lived, she'd have been about Owen's age now. That had been part of his soft spot for his boss's twins. He didn't get to raise his own girl, but he was a part of these kids' lives, and they'd taken to him. It was an honor to be trusted, to be thought of as their uncle.

"It's not that weird." Owen barked out a laugh. "But I'm not sure what I'm gonna do."

"Is she pregnant?"

"No!" Owen shot Hank an incredulous look.

"Then it's less complicated than you think. What happened?"

"I went up to the water tower with the guys, and Chloe texted us and said that she was bored. So we drove down to her ranch—"

"Her father's ranch," Hank corrected him.

"Yeah, well, she said she could come out with us, so we swung by to pick her up, and it was, like, 11, I think…"

This story sounded lengthy, and Hank crossed his arms and waited. Owen would get to it eventually.

"So Chloe was saying there was this guy who was creeping her out at school. He kept following her around and putting these creepy notes in her locker. And she doesn't like him…at all. So we said we'd get him off her back for her. So we drove past his place—"

"His parents' place," Hank corrected him again.

"Yeah, well, so he lives in that subdivision on the west end of Hope, you know with all the old trees, but everyone's been renovating and all that…"

"Yeah, I know the area."

"There was the big Dumpster outside the house because they're ripping out a bunch of old carpet and all that, so we tried to pull out some old carpet, but we couldn't get up there—"

"What did you do?" Hank had a bad feeling about this.

"We were pulling some tree branches out of the Dumpster, and we tossed one and it went harder than we thought… It broke the front window."

"Who threw it?" Hank asked.

Owen licked his lips. "Me."

"Got it." Hank sucked in a breath.

Owen eyed him cautiously for a moment. "So…"

"I'm not the one who broke someone's window." Hank shrugged. "What are you going to do?"

"I don't know." Owen shook his head. "The guy's a creep. He started some rumor at school that me and Olivia are adopted. Which is dumb, but he's that kind of guy. He's a loser…"

"So this is about you, then—"

"No, I'm just saying that it isn't just her. But he's in, like, three of her classes, so he figures he has a shot with her."

"But you do, not him?" Hank raised an eyebrow.

"Yeah, maybe I do." Owen's tone got slightly cockier. "Who'd she text when she needed help?"

Hank smiled wryly. "Here's the thing. If you got caught, you could have been charged with all sorts of misdemeanors, not to mention this is bullying. You don't like the guy, so you and a pack of friends go to his home and break his window."

"It wasn't like that!" Owen retorted.

"Sort of was," Hank replied. "Looks that way from the outside, at least. And all this was for a girl who wouldn't open her mouth and stand up for herself."

"He was creepy—"

"Yeah, you said that. But there was probably a better way to deal with it than to go to his house somewhere close to midnight."

"This is why I didn't want to say anything." Owen shot him an annoyed glare. "I don't need to be lectured. Dad could have done that."

Fine. The kid had a point. Hank took off his hat and ran a hand through his hair.

"There are two kinds of girls out there," Hank said. "Actually, three. There are the girls who aren't interested, and that's good to know. Because if she isn't into you, you just have to let it go. Like our friend the creep is going to learn. Then, of the girls who are interested, there are the ones who bring drama into your life and the ones who don't. Simple as that."

"Meaning?" Owen dug the toe of his boot into the floor.

"Meaning, Chloe is the kind who brings drama. She could have told her dad that there was a guy giving her grief. She could have told a teacher. Instead, she sneaked out of her place and drove around town with a truck full of guys from school. Then she got you all to fight her battles for her."

He knew that type of girl, because he'd married her. It never got better. Vickie was fueled by drama, and if she wasn't flirting with guys at the Honky Tonk, she was fighting with him. People got older, but their basic makeup didn't change.

"He's a creep!" Owen was exasperated now.

"Yeah," Hank said. "And you're a vandal. Everyone looks real bad in this! Except that I know you, and you aren't this kind of guy. Not normally. But if you start doing stuff to impress this girl, I'm telling you, it isn't gonna end well. You aren't her hero. She's just manipulating you."

"You don't know her."

Hank laughed softly. "Owen, there are some people who haven't gotten their act together yet. It doesn't mean that they're bad human beings, it just means that they aren't good at the relationship thing, at least not yet. And nothing good comes from trying to fix them. You just need to keep walking and find someone who doesn't leave drama in their wake."

Vickie had been the damaged one in their relationship, but after the divorce he'd realized that he wasn't quite so fresh and unbroken himself anymore. He was scarred and carried a whole lot of baggage. Compared to a woman like Avery, he was the wrecked one. So he wasn't without sympathy, either.

"It isn't her fault, though," Owen said.

"Are you happy right now?" Hank asked, changing tack.

"What?" Owen frowned.

"Are you happy?" Hank asked. "Right now. What are you feeling?"

"Kind of stressed out, I guess."

"Well, if she doesn't make you happy, walk away before you're any more invested. Cut your losses. Nice girls don't need the drama—they'll actually like you for you."

Owen didn't answer, but Hank didn't really expect him to. Owen would think it through over the next few days. It was how he worked. Teenage boys couldn't be rushed in their mental processes.

"So nice girls—like that cook." A small smile turned up one corner of Owen's lips. Was Owen seriously setting his sights on a grown woman?

"What?" Hank demanded. "She's way too old for you, kid."

She was also very likely his sister—not that he could tell him that...

"Not for me, man." Owen grinned—he'd found Hank's button. "But I've seen *you* with her."

That jarred him. When? And what exactly had he seen? Hank had thought he'd kept things under control. If Owen mentioned this to his father—

"In that scenario, I'm the one who's no good for her," Hank retorted. He was the guy who hadn't figured out relationships yet, who did everything he could to keep his wife and still failed. He was the one with a soured outlook, and she was the innocent who still saw beauty and possibility, who still believed in love. Owen was looking at him skeptically, and Hank heaved a sigh. "Besides, there are rules around here that I take pretty seriously. I'm not getting involved with another employee. There's right and there's wrong, Owen. Now go pay for that window."

"Yeah, yeah…" Owen turned toward the door. "Thanks, Uncle Hank."

Hank stood there in the hay-scented air, a bag of ranch supplies still in his hand. Some lessons were more painful than others, and Owen was going to learn his fair share of them. The kid was feeling things for this girl that were only going to lead him in the wrong direction. Hank had been there before, and now he was on the other end of that equation…

An image of Avery was stuck in his mind—that fair skin, the direct green gaze… She was an untainted woman who wanted a fairy tale that he couldn't deliver. There was no way this could end well for him…so why was he still thinking about her? Some advice was easier dished out than taken.

Chapter Nine

The following day, after breakfast was finished and the dining room had emptied, Avery stood in the middle of the kitchen. Everything had changed for her since she'd arrived in this little Montana town. While this new insight into her mother's early life didn't alter how much she loved her mom or her respect for her, it did change the story that she'd grown up with, and stories mattered.

Every family had a story, one that shaped their collective identity. She couldn't count how many times her mother had said to her, *Avery, we are Southerlys, and Southerlys don't lie. Southerlys can do hard things, Avery. And when they get knocked down, they stand back up again. So don't forget who you are and who you came from.*

The Southerlys—they had a story, and that story began with a single mother intent on giving her daughter more than she'd had growing up. Her mother had been raised by a maiden aunt, but Winona wanted Avery to have more than that—a real mother. Winona stood strong when it came to right and wrong. She'd march right back to the grocery store if she'd been undercharged for something. *We're Southerlys, Avery. We're nothing if we're not honest.*

That identity had been a bedrock for Avery. She knew who she was, what it meant to be a Southerly. When Avery was faced with a moral dilemma, her mother's voice would ring in the back of her mind— *We're Southerlys, Avery...* She always knew what she had to do, and it was never the easy way out.

Except the Southerlys weren't exactly an honorable lineage. Winona's mother gave her up at birth to a distant aunt. When Avery looked into it before her mother's death, it actually appeared that the "aunt" wasn't a family connection so much as a friend of the family, and there was a whole ugly story about Winona's parents having spent some time in prison. There wasn't a deluge of Southerlys to confirm her mother's adamant declarations of what kind of person constituted a Southerly. It was one woman's word against the world.

Avery plunged her rubber-gloved hands into the hot water to get started on the dishes. It was a startling thing to find out that her mother hadn't always been the woman she'd known. When had things changed—at Avery's birth? It was possible. Winona'd walked away from Hope, Montana, and she'd given birth in a different state, started a whole new life. She'd even walked away from the father of her baby...

And now she knew why. If Winona had stayed here, she'd have been under the weight of her reputation. And the Southerlys knew a whole lot about bad reputations, it seemed. Some fresh starts required clean breaks, and she couldn't imagine the kind of strength it had taken for an eighteen-year-old girl to move to a new state, give birth and completely reinvent herself. Because the Winona Southerly of Hope, Montana, was a different woman from the Winona Southerly of Salina, Kansas.

We are Southerlys, Avery, and we don't do anything we're not willing to have the entire world know about. So think before you act, sweetheart. What you do when no one is looking defines you.

Avery wiped down a ladle, then rinsed it with the sprayer. Once the kitchen was clean, she'd have some time to herself before she started in on dinner. Tonight would be chicken legs, rice and vegetables. Nothing too complicated, but she still felt a leap in her stomach when she thought about all that could go wrong.

Last night, she'd seriously considered going back home to Kansas. Did she really want to uproot a man's life just so she could feel better about knowing who her father was? She'd gone so far as to pull out her suitcase and start throwing in her clothes, but then she'd stopped.

Another few days wouldn't hurt. Another chance to talk to her dad… Another view into her mother's world… If she left now, she'd be going without completing the goal she'd set for herself. She'd come to Montana for a reason, and she'd never forgive herself if she gave up because she was afraid.

We are Southerlys, and we can do hard things. Don't forget who you are and who you came from.

Her mother had declared who they were—without any actual ancestral support. She had decided who they would be from that point on. They were Southerlys, and Winona was choosing something better—nobility, honesty, integrity. And God help the person who contradicted that.

So staying and confronting her dad wouldn't be easy, but since when did Southerlys choose the easy road?

Avery reached into the sudsy water again and slid her gloved hand over the bottom of the sink, looking for any last large utensils. At first she didn't feel pain—it was more like a tug, and then a sting. When she pulled her hand out of the water, she saw a slice in the yellow rubber glove and a watery wash of blood.

"Blast it…" Her head spun and she leaned forward to catch her balance. She eased her hand out of the rubber, and shook off the other glove, then clamped down on her finger to stop the bleeding. It couldn't be that bad, could it? Like paper cuts that bled a lot…

She grabbed a kitchen towel and put it on top of the cut. It hurt—a lot. After a moment, blood soaked through the towel, and her stomach roiled with the pain. This was no paper cut. Was she going to need stitches?

She had no idea where the hospital was, and her head was swimming too much to be much use. She let go of the cut hand in order to grab her cell phone, and as she did, the blood started flowing again in earnest.

She selected Hank's phone number, then pinched her phone between her shoulder and cheek so she could put the pressure back onto that cut.

"Avery?" In the background, she could hear some heavy machinery running.

"Hi, Hank." Her voice didn't sound as strong as she hoped.

"You okay?" She could hear his concern.

"I cut myself. You gave me your number for emergencies, and while I'm not exactly on death's door here, I thought I should probably tell you." She laughed weakly. "There's probably a form for that, right?"

"How bad is the cut?" he asked.

"Well…" She pulled back the towel and grimaced at the gape of red in her flesh across the tip of her finger. "Pretty bad."

"Okay, I'm on my way."

"Wait—" Was this really worth calling in the boss? Toughened ranch workers probably did this sort of thing on a regular basis, and Southerlys weren't wimps. "I mean, how far away are you? This is probably not that big of a deal. I just need to sit down for a minute."

She could probably live without a fingertip.

"I'm not far," he said. "Don't worry about it. I'll be there soon. I take my paperwork very seriously."

He hung up on his end, and she let the phone drop to the countertop next to her. She felt better knowing that he was on his way.

SAYING THAT HE wasn't far away was a lie, but Hank had heard the pain and panic in her voice the minute she'd spoken. His men knew their work, so he gave a couple of last-minute instructions to the team leader, then headed for his truck.

The day was hot and high cumulus clouds scudded across the pale blue sky. He drove with his window down, stepping on the gas so that billows of dust rose up behind him, blotting out the road in the rearview mirror.

He'd been thinking about Avery all day, going over

what his cousin had said about her mother. He hated that she had to learn about her mother that way. She was embarrassed, and while he'd wanted to support her, she'd pulled away, closed off.

That was why he'd told her about Vickie and the baby—he'd wanted her to know that she mattered to her parents. Her sense of value had taken a hit, and the thought that her existence should be less of a celebration because her mother hadn't known what she wanted as a teenager...that was just insulting, to all of them.

The drive from the far field took about fifteen minutes. It would have taken twenty-five if he'd driven at a reasonable speed. He pulled up beside the canteen and parked, then hopped out. He sincerely hoped that she wasn't hurt too badly and he wouldn't be driving her to the hospital, but he was ready to if needed.

He pulled open the front door and wove through the tables toward the kitchen.

"Avery?" He pushed open the swinging door and saw her leaning against the counter, an open first-aid kit in front of her and a bloody rubber glove next to it.

"Hi, Hank." She lifted a hand covered in a dish towel. "I've had an adventure."

"Yeah, looks like. Let me wash my hands first." The last thing she needed was an infection. He scrubbed his hands, then dried them and headed back to where she stood. Her hair was loose around her shoulders, and she looked paler than usual, her lips white.

"Alright. Let's have a look." He pulled back the towel and frowned. It was a pretty bad cut. The bleeding had slowed considerably, though, and clotting had started. This would definitely hurt.

"Do you want stitches?" he asked.

"Not really," she replied. "Do you think I need them?"

"I've seen worse. It's up to you," he replied. "I can do my best to bandage you up here, or I can take you to the hospital and get a couple of stitches in that to hold it together."

Avery shook her head, swallowed hard. "No, patch me up here."

"Come out to a table," he said, gathering up the first-aid kit in one hand and taking her elbow with the other. "You look ready to faint."

"I'm not," she said weakly, but her pallor said something different.

"Alright," he said. "Still, let's get you sitting down."

Hank flicked on some lights and pulled out a chair at the nearest table for her. She sat down and Hank took a seat next to her, pulling out gauze, bandages and some ointment.

"I was talking to Mr. Harmon this morning," Hank said. He removed the towel once more and smoothed his hand across her forearm. "Relax, okay?"

She relaxed her fingers, but winced. "What did he have to say?"

It looked like she was willing to be distracted while he worked, so he kept talking. "He still thought you might be interested in meeting Chris Mayfield. I go to church every week, and I thought you might want to come along."

He applied some ointment to the cut flesh and then

pushed it together. She grimaced but didn't pull back. He didn't want to hurt her, telling himself it would hurt a whole lot less once he was done and the wound wasn't gaping in the air.

"Does Mr. Harmon go, too?" she asked.

"Yup."

"Church with the family," she murmured.

What was Avery picturing right now? He knew what he was thinking about—a chance to spend a day with her. Sundays were generally a day off around here, and the cook's duties were considerably lighter. He wanted to ignore the service and just have her next to him for an hour. Stupid, maybe, but it was what he wanted. She wasn't going to be here for long, and he just wanted a little bit of time with her before she left. Stupid? Perhaps, but honest.

"You could also see it as a chance to see Louis and the kids all together," he added. Was he trying to convince her to go? He cut a piece of gauze and wrapped it around the cut on her finger, then reached for bandage tape.

"I don't know if I'd get the cleanup done in time after breakfast," she said.

"Sunday morning is cold cereal and muffins," Hank said with a shrug. "Everyone fends for themselves for lunch. And after breakfast, I'll give you a hand with the cleanup."

She smiled at that, then shot him an amused look. "You want me there?"

"Sure." He smiled, but kept his attention on bandaging up the finger. "Is that too tight?"

"No, it's fine." She paused, watching as he pushed down the last of the tape. "Would it be weird, though?"

"I don't think so. You'd be with me."

She nodded. "Okay."

Her agreement made him feel mildly victorious. He held up her hand and examined his work. "Done. What do you think?"

"It feels better. Thanks." She pulled her hand back, then looked at him. "How often does this happen?"

"More often than you'd think." He gave her a reassuring smile. "I mean, less often in the kitchen, but…"

She rolled her eyes. "It's harder than it looks in here, you know."

"I know." He had to hold himself back from reaching out and touching her. What was it about those fiery curls and the freckles scattered across her face that softened him like this? Any other cook—any other woman—and he'd be able to keep himself in check easily enough. "Look, about yesterday—"

"I should have talked to Hillary alone," she interrupted. "Sorry to have dragged you into that."

That wasn't what he was getting at. He knew she'd been embarrassed, but maybe it was good that he'd seen it, because at least he understood what she was going through. Of all people in Hope, he understood…

"Here's the thing," Hank said. "This town has a long memory. Not much happens around here, so people gossip. It's all they've got. And trust me, I know all about that. My divorce is still the subject of conversation."

Avery pulled her unbandaged hand through her hair,

tugging the waves and curls away from her face. "Mom completely reinvented herself in Kansas. Completely."

"We all do that at some point," Hank replied. "We change things, decide who we want to be."

"Have you?" she asked.

"Of course." He shrugged. "I used to be a noble guy. You don't know my cousin, Chet Granger, but he was in love with his wife for years and wouldn't do anything about it because his younger brother had dated her. We were raised to do the right thing—even if it hurt."

"Chet obviously got the girl," she observed.

"Yeah, eventually," Hank agreed. "I stood by my girlfriend. My uncles told me they were proud of me, what a good guy I was, and I liked that. But the thing was, marrying her might have been popular in everyone else's opinions, but it was no good for me or for Vickie. We were miserable together."

He could still remember the glowing comments from his family. *She's lucky to have you. Any other guy might have walked away. You're a good man, Hank. If only more men stood up and took responsibility like you do...* And all those comments and back pats had made a difference. If it weren't for the constant encouragement, he might have backed out and saved himself and Vickie a whole lot of grief.

"And so you stopped being the noble guy?" Was that disappointment he saw in her face?

"Yeah..." He nodded, then shrugged apologetically. "After she left, I looked back on all the choices I'd made and I realized that I went against my gut and I did what other people would approve of. I'll never do that again."

"My mother went the other direction," Avery said. "She cared a lot what others thought."

"I guess that's the point I'm trying to make. Public opinion is a powerful thing, especially in a town this small," he said. "I know that as well as your mom did."

Avery nodded. "Which is why I'm not going to be good news, Hank."

He hadn't meant that…but he could see her point. In a town like Hope, these kinds of surprises greased the rumor mill for years. But the thought of her feeling rejected already—that tugged at his heart.

"Avery, you're good news to me." His voice was low and gruff. He wasn't used to putting his feelings into words, and he shook his head, trying to sort out how to say this. "I mean…I know why you came here, but when you arrived, life just got more interesting. For me, at least. You're beautiful and funny, and you've got this really determined drive, even when anyone else would have given up. Not you. So who cares what the town thinks of you? I like you. A lot… And I'm glad you're burning our food."

Avery chuckled at his last line, and he smiled, too. "Seriously."

"You're very sweet, Hank." Her eyes misted.

"Yeah, I try…" He rose to his feet and held out a hand to her. She took his fingers and stood up, but as she did, he found her closer than expected. She was right there, inches from him, her face tipped up toward his in an expression of surprise. Her lips parted, and she looked ready to take a step back, but he didn't want her to move away… He slid his hand around her waist, feeling the warmth of her body against his palm, and tugged her against him.

I could get fired for this...

She didn't resist. He knew he could have stopped— released her, walked away—but it would have taken a whole lot more strength than he had right then. He splayed his fingers across her back, then lowered his lips onto hers.

Her mouth was even softer than he'd imagined it. When she leaned into him, his heart sped up and he wrapped his arms around her more firmly and deepened the kiss. She responded with a sigh that only served to fire his blood. His mind was moving ahead—past this moment and into territory where he'd vowed he'd never go again. It had been a long time since he'd done this, and he hadn't meant to break his drought with her...

No, he had to stop. He pulled back, licked his lips and let out a frustrated sigh. His body wanted a whole lot more than this...

"Sorry," he murmured. "That was really unprofessional."

"It's okay..." She swallowed, dropped her gaze and stepped away. Had he scared her? Offended her? He wasn't sure—that kiss hadn't been intentional. He'd meant to reassure her, not kiss her. And he hadn't been prepared to feel that much longing once his arms were around her slim waist.

Avery was young and in a vulnerable place right now, and the last thing she needed was to be the comfort of some broken-down cowboy. He hadn't meant to put that on her.

"So do you still want that ride to church?" he asked. Now that he'd kissed her. Now that he'd tipped that balance between them… "You can say *No*."

"I want the ride." She gave him a small smile, then turned and headed back to the kitchen. "And you promised to help me clean up, remember. I'm going to hold you to that."

Was that forgiveness? He sure hoped so, because he was already steeling himself against whatever this was he was feeling for her.

He shouldn't kiss her again—he'd be risking everything—but right now, it was all he could think about. Driving her to church was a bad idea, but it was too late to back out. He'd just have to keep himself under control.

Chapter Ten

Avery noticed that Hank kept his distance all day Saturday. He passed her once in the bunkhouse, and his warm gaze had met hers for a moment. His finger had slid across her hand on the way past…but he didn't look back. And she'd been left there feeling tingly and uncertain.

She'd been thinking about the kiss ever since it happened, going over the way he'd pulled her so solidly into his arms, the feel of his lips moving over hers… He was obviously more experienced than she was. She'd never been kissed quite like that! Not that she'd had many boyfriends, exactly…

That Sunday morning, as she gathered up the cereal boxes and loaded the plates and bowls into plastic tubs to carry into the kitchen, she lost herself in memories of the kiss again.

"Morning."

She startled as Hank came up beside her, and she glanced up to see his warm smile.

"Good morning," she answered. "I wasn't sure if you'd still come."

"I'm a man of my word," he said with a wink. "How's the finger?"

"Healing." It still throbbed a little, but it was coming along. "You're rather good at bandaging up gashes, you know."

"I've had practice," he said with a low laugh. "Here, let me take that."

His biceps flexed as he picked up the tub of dishes and headed toward the swinging kitchen door. Avery grabbed an armload of cereal boxes and followed.

Hank was indeed true to his word and helped her with all of the cleanup. He was efficient in the kitchen, and when they were done, she glanced at her watch.

"We should probably go get ready," he said. "Did you bring anything…dressy?"

"Yeah, I'll be fine."

"I should tell you…" He paused and those warm eyes met hers for a moment. "Mr. Harmon's late wife, Carla, is buried in the churchyard."

"Oh…" She let that sink in, then nodded. "Okay."

"They bring fresh flowers for her grave once a month, and this is the week they'll be doing it. Just so you know."

Avery could hear the warning between the lines. This would be a somber day for the family, and likely a time when they pulled close. It wouldn't include her—not that she expected today to be about her in any way… She wouldn't make any announcements just now.

"She was very loved, wasn't she?" she said after a beat of silence.

"She was," he agreed. Then he gave a nod. "All right, well…I'll meet you back here in ten minutes."

Avery had brought one dress with her—a light gray, knee-length cotton shift, decorated with pale pink embroidery along the neckline. It cinched at the waist with a cloth belt. As she dressed, she wondered if today was a bad day to go get a look at Chris Mayfield, when Louis and his children had such personal plans. He obviously didn't think that he was her father…but still. Why would he tell Hank that she'd need to see Chris Mayfield? Her mother had dated him off and on, Hillary had confirmed, but if Hillary was right and her mother had been with several boys her senior year, why would Louis be so insistent that she meet their pastor? Maybe Winona's female friends had known more about her love life than Louis had.

Ten minutes later, as promised, Hank pulled up in front of the bunkhouse where Avery waited.

"You look nice," Hank said through the open window. He was wearing a blue plaid button-up shirt and a clean cowboy hat, and it looked like he'd had a fresh shave, too. "Hop in."

She headed around to the passenger side and he leaned over to push open the door for her. She climbed in and got settled as Hank put the truck into gear.

"You clean up nicely," she said as she clicked the seat belt into place.

"I'm capable of being presentable," he said with a grin. "But cows aren't that picky, and neither are ranch hands."

She smiled at his joke. "So how come you go with the Harmons to church every week?"

"I don't drink," he said.

"What?" She frowned.

"I'm ranch manager, which means that I'm pretty much on call 24/7. I don't get an actual break unless I get off the ranch and turn off my cell phone for a while. Most guys do that at the bar, but I don't drink."

"Oh…" She nodded. "But church?"

"Faith matters to me," he said. "Besides, it's quiet, I like stained glass, I can think my own thoughts uninterrupted. But there is the social aspect, too. I get to catch up with people I wouldn't see too often otherwise. I'm single—I need the connection. Do you know what I mean?"

"Actually, I do," she agreed. "It can get lonely."

Hank turned from the gravel of the ranch road onto asphalt. As the truck sped up, she put up her window to keep her hair from blowing around and settled back into the seat for the ride. Hank stepped on the gas and the engine rumbled beneath them. A Sunday drive felt different, somehow…more relaxing, less pressure. They drove in silence for several minutes, and she watched the scenery loping past her window: cows, pasture, the odd sagging barn. Hope wasn't too far away, and soon the first outlying buildings began to appear.

"The local restaurants must like Sundays," she commented.

"You bet," Hank said with a shrug. "Most of the ranches around here run the same way. Gives the cooks a break, and gives the restaurants some business."

"Sounds like a system that benefits everyone," she agreed. She could use the break, too.

"I'm going riding this afternoon," Hank added. "Another way to get away from it all for a while. Do you ride?"

"Not much," she admitted. "I've gone on a few trail rides, but I'm not sure that counts."

"You'll have about two hours between church and when you need to start dinner," he said. "If you want to come with me, you're welcome."

Riding—it had been a while since she'd been on a horse, and the company of this handsome cowboy certainly sweetened the deal. Avery glanced over at him—his hand resting on the top of the steering wheel, his hat pushed back on his head. She wasn't here for much longer. The clock was running out before she needed to be back in Kansas for the reopening of Winona's Wilderness. And she'd miss Hank, she realized. She'd really miss him. Somehow, she'd gotten attached to this gruff cowboy, and then he'd kissed her, and…

Avery wasn't supposed to be feeling these things. She'd come here for a reason, and getting entangled with some guy wasn't a part of that. Her mother had shown her how to live with purpose. She wouldn't get involved with men when she knew it couldn't last. She owed herself that much.

"Unless you'd be uncomfortable," he said when she hadn't answered for a moment. "I know I overstepped the other day in the dining room. I shouldn't have. I'm your boss, and you're here for your own reasons…" His voice trailed off and he looked away for a moment, his expression hidden.

That was part of what had been nagging at her ever since that kiss—why? What had it meant, if anything?

"How come you kissed me?" she asked.

He sighed. "I don't know. I guess it was all those little things… The way your lips part when you draw a breath, the way your cheeks get all pink every time you're the slightest bit uncomfortable… And I like your freckles, following them down your neck, across your collarbones. You're beautiful, but more than that. You're… God, I don't know. You're just you. And I had you that close… I just…kissed you."

She'd never heard a man describe her that way before— the things that made her a little shy about herself, like her freckles, had drawn him in.

"I did kiss you back," she admitted, feeling the heat rise in her cheeks again, the way he'd described her.

"Yeah, I know." He cast her a slight smile. "And I've been thinking about doing it again."

So had she, but she knew better than to start something she couldn't finish. She wasn't the casual dating sort—her heart got involved too easily.

"I'm going to talk to Louis soon—I promised three days, remember?"

"Yeah."

"I'm not around here for much longer. We both know it…"

"And if we were caught, I'd be fired on the spot."

"I don't want to get attached—" she swallowed "—to

you, I mean. I don't want to feel things like this… I just
want to stay focused on my reason for being here, and
then go back home and reopen the shop."

"Yeah," he repeated.

"So…" *How to say this…* "We shouldn't do that…
the kissing, I mean."

She sounded like an idiot, and she knew it. She knew
what she wanted, and feeling like this just got in the way.
Maybe this was how her mother felt with the guys she'd
been with—attracted, so very attracted, even though
there was no future. And she was her mother's daughter, because there was something about this cowboy in
this blasted town that tempted her like she'd never been
tempted before.

"Okay." He reached over and took her hand—his
firm, calloused grip moving gently over fingers, stopping at the bandage. "I won't kiss you again."

Was that a promise she wanted to hear? Not really,
but it was better to have some ground rules. Falling for
him wasn't part of the plan.

Hank signaled and released her hand to crank the
wheel. Avery could see the church across the fields—
white siding, with a steeple.

Buried in a churchyard where a devoted husband
and children brought flowers…this could have been her
mother's legacy if she'd only told Louis the truth, that he
was the father of her unborn baby. If Hank was the kind
of man to stand by the mother of his child, then Louis
would have done the right thing, too. Both of their lives
would have been much different. Except then Carla and

Louis wouldn't have had their loving marriage, and the twins never would have been born... Maybe too many things would have been different.

They pulled into a parking space and Hank turned off the motor. Avery's gaze was drawn to a man standing by the open church doors, shaking hands with parishioners as they went inside. He was tall, fit and looked to be in his midforties. He smiled and bent down to say something to an elderly woman, shaking her hand as they spoke.

"Oh, my goodness..." she murmured.

"Yeah..." Hank sighed. "That's Pastor Mayfield, and that's probably why Louis wanted you to meet him so badly."

Chris Mayfield had a head full of dark red hair. It wasn't as fiery as Avery's, closer to an auburn and graying at the temples, but most definitely red. She hadn't noticed that in the photos of him, hadn't been looking closely...

Could her mother have been mistaken?

HANK STAYED NEXT to Avery during the service, standing and sitting with the rest of the congregation. They arrived later than the Harmons did, and the pew next to Louis and the kids was already filled, so they sat a couple of rows ahead. He'd found comfort in the routine and the structure of a church service in the past, but today none of it seemed to be working. His mind was firmly on her... The way her dress smoothed over her leg, the way the light from the stained glass windows played across her pale hands. She sat a modest six inches away from him, which had somehow made all of it worse. He couldn't stop thinking about closing that gap—sliding an arm around her, feeling her against him.

Except they were in church with Louis and his kids sitting a couple of rows back. Avery had turned around a couple of times already, glancing back at the Harmons, but Hank kept his eyes forward and cursed himself for encouraging this to begin with. Obviously, he hadn't thought it all the way through.

Once the sermon started, Avery's focus turned to the pastor, but her gaze was fixed a little too firmly to Chris Mayfield for her interest to be spiritual. Hank wondered what she was feeling, thinking…but obviously, couldn't ask.

When the service ended, they trailed out of the church with everyone else. Louis and the kids went to the graveyard. Owen put a bouquet of daisies next to the headstone. Louis stood in the center, with his children on either side of him. Hank never intruded on those quiet moments when the four of them were together again. He wondered what it would be like to have had a life filled with so much love that even death didn't completely separate them.

"You said they do this every month?" Avery asked softly.

Hank nodded. "Like clockwork. But even on the weeks when they don't bring flowers, Louis goes down to her grave for a few minutes."

He'd overheard Louis talking to her once, his hand on the gravestone and his voice choked with tears.

"Will he ever get over her?" Avery asked.

Hank thought for a moment, then shook his head. "Not completely. If he moves on, the next woman will have to understand that part of his heart will always be Carla's. They were a once-in-a-lifetime kind of thing."

Avery was silent for a moment, and he glanced over at her. A breeze ruffled her tangled curls, and sadness welled up in her eyes.

"Mom deserved that," she murmured.

"Your mom had that," he countered. "In you."

But he knew what Avery meant. Everyone wanted the kind of romance that Louis and Carla had shared— even Hank. Who didn't long for passion and commitment that didn't fizzle out? He'd given it his best shot with Vickie, but it seemed like the kind of love that went the distance couldn't be forced or planned. All the good behavior in the world couldn't conjure it up.

"You ready to go?" Hank asked, and Avery pulled her gaze away from the graveyard and nodded.

"Let's go," she agreed.

Hank was eager to ride, to get away from prying eyes. That was normally how he sorted out his feelings—on the wide-open plains where the wind made the grass ripple like the sea. And he'd invited Avery...

Sitting next to her in church was proof that bringing her to his personal escape wasn't a good idea. Avery was the source of a lot of his knotted emotions, and having her with him wasn't going to help matters...except that he knew her time here was short, and he wanted to make the most of it. It was selfish, and he knew it. He should be letting her discuss her situation with Mr. Harmon…

"So do you want to come for the ride?" Hank asked. "I know you wanted to talk to Mr. Harmon."

"I'm not procrastinating," she said quietly. "I'm just…" She sighed. "I'm hoping a good moment will present itself. If not, I'll have to force it. If you think you need to tell him…"

"No." Hank sighed. "That's between you and the boss. I'm not a part of it. I just want to make sure you do tell him."

"It's why I came. But he's just been to his wife's grave, and…"

The timing was bad. Hank could see that, too.

"If you don't want me to come—"

"No, it's not that—" And it wasn't. He wanted her to come along too badly—that was the problem. This was dangerous territory. "Sure. Let's ride. Give the family some time today."

This would be a goodbye—something to remember on long, lonely nights checking on herds. It had been a long time since he'd felt anything like this for a woman. He wasn't deluding himself into thinking that this was anything more than a friendship fraught with inappropriate attraction, but he'd have time enough to purge her from his system once she was gone.

They got into the truck and Hank pulled out onto the dirt road that headed back toward the highway.

"A love like that is inspiring," Avery said, rolling

down her window to let the air blow her hair away from her face.

Inspiring…in a way. It was also daunting, and frustratingly out of reach.

"Their marriage is part of the reason I don't want to get married again," Hank confessed.

"Why?" She shot him an odd look. "I thought you said they were happy."

"They were," he agreed. "Really happy. They were the kind of couple everyone wanted to be like. They thoroughly enjoyed each other. They laughed at each other's jokes, finished each other's sentences. Even the things that annoyed them about each other turned into endearing qualities. I remember him telling me that she could never buy him a gift that he'd like. A lot of guys would find that irritating, opening gifts year after year that never hit the mark, but not him. He thought it was kind of sweet because she'd try so hard to find just the right thing. The fact that she failed at it made him all the more protective of her feelings."

"He loved her," Avery said.

"They had a great life," he agreed. "But unattainable to everyday Joes like me."

"How do you know?" she countered.

"I was raised a good country boy," Hank said. "You're supposed to be able to reap what you sow. If you put in carrot seeds, you get carrots. If you put in flower seeds, you get flowers. Well, I put in a lot of hard work, dedication. I didn't flirt with other women, and I did everything I could think of to make my wife happy. When you put a woman first in your life, you're supposed to see that reflected in the relationship. But it didn't work like that. She still wasn't happy. I put down seeds and nothing came up."

He could remember taking her out for dinner near the end, and they'd just sat there in the restaurant and stared at each other. They had nothing to say. They made small talk, and he couldn't wait to pay the bill and get out of there. What was so wrong with them that they couldn't even shoot the breeze? Whatever Mr. Harmon had with his wife—that sparkle they shared—had eluded him and Vickie from the start.

"She wasn't the right one for you," Avery said.

"That's for sure," he said. "But I was raised by people who said that romance and butterflies only took a couple so far, and after that it came down to hard work. I thought if I only worked hard enough, it would succeed."

When he'd confided in his dad how things were going with Vickie, he'd told him that the honeymoon was over. It was time to roll up his sleeves.

"That sounds wise to me," she replied.

"My dad even told me that when he married Mom, it wasn't because he thought she was the prettiest girl or because she made him feel like a bull in the spring. He married her for other reasons."

"Like what?" she asked.

"She was practical, good with money, loyal and grew the heartiest garden he'd ever seen."

And Hank's mother did grow a fantastic garden. Her

cucumbers outproduced anyone else's, and her gourds were the size of watermelons.

"That's it?" Avery asked with a low laugh. "Not quite what a woman wants to hear…"

"Well, they also were the only two single people in the church they attended, and they both wanted to get married and start a family. Her father said that if my dad married my mom, he'd give them a down payment for his garage in town. So that factored in, too."

His parents' story was far from romantic, and it wasn't one that they tended to tell too often. They'd been hard-working people who got married, had five children and just kept on working hard.

"Are they happy?" Avery asked dubiously. "Is your mom okay with that?"

"Yes. That's the thing." Hank slowed for a turn. "With that kind of start, you'd think they'd have been divorced in five years, but they stuck with it. They never were the lovey-dovey kind of couple in public, but they had each other's backs. No matter what. And over the years, they grew to truly love and respect each other."

"So…it kind of worked out," Avery concluded.

"You could say so," Hank agreed. "They're now in Florida together where my father is collecting stamps and my mother is trying to figure out how to bake bread in their Airstream. So if my parents, with a marriage so practical it was almost painful, could stay together quite contentedly because they put in the hard work, then why couldn't I make my marriage with Vickie go the distance?"

Hank slowed to turn again, this time down the road that lead to Harmon Ranch. He knew the route like the back of his hand, and his truck almost drove it by itself. Some grazing cattle looked up, slowly chewing, tufts of grass sticking out the sides of their mouths.

"Do you miss Vickie?" Avery asked after a few beats of silence.

It wasn't that he was still heartbroken over Vickie— he was gun-shy. She'd shown him his shortcomings and his weaknesses.

"No..." Hank shook his head, and he slowed to drive around a pothole in the gravel road, then sped up as he passed it. "It's been five years, and I honestly don't miss her, exactly, but I did wonder for a long time where I went wrong... My parents' marriage advice didn't do the trick—hard work didn't make up the difference like it had for them. And they certainly hadn't started out with any great spark of magic."

"So what did Carla and Louis have?" Avery twisted in her seat to look at him, and he glanced at her out of the corner of his eye.

"That's the question. I don't even know. They had physical attraction, some chemistry...but you give it enough years and that will wane, too." He shrugged. "I do think they had something special, but how do you quantify that? How do you know if you've found it?"

"So you don't like the risk," she concluded.

"Bingo." He shot her a grin. "I've been divorced once, and I don't think I could survive it a second time. There is no formula that makes for a happy marriage that I can see."

"You need a formula?"

"Yup."

And maybe he did at this point. He'd tried trusting good intentions, he'd even married the mother of his child. When a man did everything right and his marriage still failed, he knew better than to try again. Maybe he was the one who was missing something—some vital ingredient that made a woman want to stick around.

Avery laughed softly. "You're an interesting man, Hank."

"That's why I tend to keep my mouth shut and just ride," Hank said. "No explanations needed that way."

Except that he had wanted to explain…he wanted Avery to understand, and he wasn't even sure why. He'd made his peace with being single a few years ago, but there was a small part of him that still longed for something more. He just didn't trust that he'd get it.

Times were different now. People didn't get married for practical purposes—they wanted the real thing, and if they missed the mark, they tried again. In an eventual parting of the ways, someone got trampled and left behind.

"Is it okay to be content?" Hank asked. "Is it okay to be with someone and think, *This isn't so bad*?"

"That's not what I want," Avery replied. "I want love and passion, romance that grows over time. I want the real thing."

"Yeah, I get it." He took the last turn onto the ranch

property. He didn't blame her, but he didn't want that, either. Not again. "Sometimes, contentedness is as good as it gets."

It had been for his parents, and it was the same for him and Vickie. It was better to just stay single and not inflict himself for the long-term onto anyone else. He pulled up to a stop in front of the bunkhouse.

"So you coming to ride?" he asked.

She regarded him for a moment, and he wondered what she thought of him.

"Alright," she said at last. "Just let me get changed."

He couldn't help the smile that came to his lips. It would never work—they were both pretty clear on that—but he wanted some time with her, anyway.

Chapter Eleven

Avery sat astride the chestnut mare and brushed her hands down her jean-clad thighs. They'd packed a quick lunch from the kitchen, then went to the barn to saddle up. Her mount, Pickles, stood in the center of the paddock. From her vantage point, she could see down some rolling hills with grazing cattle. Blocks of field and pasture lay side by side, patched together by lines of barbed wire fence. The blue sky sparkled with sunlight, faint wisps of cloud floating high overhead, and on the breeze she could hear the twitter of birdsong and the far-off growl of a tractor's engine.

"Coming?" Hank called. He was at the paddock gate, mounted on a dappled stallion that pranced impatiently.

"Let's go, Pickles," Avery said, and gave the horse a little kick in the sides. Pickles took one step forward, then stopped.

"What's wrong?" Hank chuckled.

"Nothing," she replied. "Pickles, let go!"

"Let her know who's boss," Hank said.

"How, exactly?" she asked incredulously. "She isn't buying it!"

Hank made a clicking sound with his mouth and Pickles trotted obediently toward him. Obviously Hank was boss around here, and Avery was perfectly fine with that. As long as Pickles listened to someone.

Her horse stopped at Hank's side and he shot her a grin. "You going to be okay?"

"Don't worry about me," she replied. "It's just nice to be out of the kitchen."

Hank led the way, swinging the gate closed after them. They went down a gravel road, horse hooves clopping at a soothing pace.

"So you don't like cooking at all?" Hank asked, glancing over at her.

"I cook for necessity," she replied. Here at Harmon ranch, she was cooking for a chance to tell her father who she was…if her mother hadn't been wrong. "Why—do you like cooking?"

"Yeah. Not for thirty-five men, mind you." He adjusted his hat on his head. "I make a particularly good cream soup, though."

Avery couldn't help the smile the came to her mouth. "Are you serious?"

"Deadly." He arched an eyebrow.

"How come you never told me this before?"

"I thought I'd made it clear that I knew my way around a kitchen."

And perhaps he had, but still…

He grinned. "I also make a chocolate cheesecake that would curl your toes."

She smiled at that mental image and she had no doubt he was telling the truth.

"Any chance you'd cook for me?" she asked.

"If there's time."

His words knocked the flirtatious sizzle from the air. He was right—she wasn't sticking around. This was a very temporary situation, and the flower shop was waiting for her back in Salina, filled with the memories of her mother and her childhood. She looked forward to stocking it with flowers again, to putting out the clapboard with her mother's carefully painted welcome sign. Her mother had worked too hard to build that business for Avery to sell it to a stranger... It needed to stay in the family. The shop was all she had left of her mom... and yet she'd been forgetting that lately when she and Hank were together. She felt a flood of guilt.

"So what did you think of Chris?" Hank asked.

"The fact that he has red hair, you mean," she said. He didn't answer, and she sighed. "I'd hate to be wrong."

Hank led the way north and they cut into a field of lush grass. He kicked his gelding's sides and sped up into a trot. Pickles followed without any prompting from Avery and she gasped, leaning forward to regain her balance. The bouncing was slightly more intimidating, but when she let her hips move with the rhythm of her horse, she found her comfort again.

"Not bad," Hank said, shooting her a grin.

"I really can't put this off any longer. Hank, could you set up a meeting between me and Louis tomorrow? I'm going to talk to him, whether the moment seems right or not."

"Yeah, I could do that," he said. "You ready?"

"I'll have to be," she replied. "If I'm opening Mom's

store next Monday, I have a lot of work to get done before that. I'll need to head back."

Hank's expression softened. "You sure you want to go?"

"Of course." It was the plan all along, wasn't it? Whatever this was they were enjoying here in Hope, it couldn't last. "I'm sorry that I'm not a long-term solution for a cook, but you'll all be happier with someone else in the kitchen, I'm sure."

"Let's just enjoy today," he said. "And I'll set something up with Louis for tomorrow morning."

"What will you do for a cook?" she asked.

"Someone will apply. I've been asking around."

That stung just a little, although it shouldn't. She'd told him she wouldn't be here long, but for some reason she didn't like to think about being so easily replaced.

"I'm sorry, you know," she said.

"For what?" he asked.

"For coming under false pretenses and all that. I've set you back on finding someone permanent."

"Mr. Harmon will understand, you can trust me on that." But his eyes were sad. "Ready to gallop?"

He didn't wait for an answer; he bent over his horse and urged him forward into a full gallop. Avery watched him sprint ahead for a moment before Pickles followed suit, and Avery's breath caught in her throat as she was launched forward. She hunched low over Pickles's back—the only way to actually stay in the saddle— and forced herself to breathe.

At first, all she could feel was panic, but then she realized that the bumping had stopped when Pickles reached her stride, and she was filled with elation. She'd never ridden a galloping horse before, and she knew she'd have to do this again.

Hank reined in ahead of her, and Pickles slowed, too. He looked back at her with a grin.

"That was amazing!" She laughed. "And a first."

"That's right—" he grimaced "—sorry, I'd forgotten… I shouldn't have—"

"The only way to learn," she said with more confidence than she felt.

"You hungry yet?" he asked.

"My stomach is back there." She hooked a thumb over her shoulder.

She earned a laugh for that one, and he met her gaze with an easy smile. Out here it felt different—freer, farther away from all the pressures. And the way Hank caught her eye…it sent her mind into the wrong direction. She hoped her shortness of breath would be attributed to the ride.

"See those trees?" Hank pointed ahead to a copse. "We can eat there in the shade."

The trees were surrounded by a wave of pink wildflowers, and their scent surfed the breeze toward them. They rode over to the shade and Hank dismounted. Avery looked down at the ground, and then considered her options.

"Need a hand?" He came up beside Pickles and took the reins.

Avery took her foot out of the stirrup, but her legs felt like jelly. Her muscles weren't used to this. But she got her leg over and she felt Hank's strong grip on her waist as she came down. Her feet hit the ground and she heaved a sigh of relief. When she turned, Hank stepped back a respectful distance, but his gaze warmed, and he smiled.

"We'll let them graze," Hank said.

While Hank saw to the horses, Avery admired a clump of wildflowers. They were lovely and fragile— the kind of blossom that wouldn't survive a truck ride to a flower shop. The most beautiful flowers were like that—too fragile to be enjoyed anywhere else but their natural habitat. Like this—whatever it was she was doing with Hank. It required this land, this air, this ranch... She was going home soon, and he would stay here.

Her stomach rumbled as they sauntered over to the shade. They sank down into the grass, and Hank opened the lunch bag. There were two sandwiches, some muffins, some apple slices and a few carrots.

"The carrots are for the horses," he said, and as if on cue, the horses came over to. "They know I'm good for it."

As the horses crunched on their treat, Avery opened the first sandwich and discovered cold cuts and cheese on a crusty bun. She didn't wait on ceremony, but took a jaw-cracking bite. The tang of pickle mingled with mayonnaise in absolute perfection. She rolled her eyes upward in appreciation.

"I also make a good sandwich," Hank said, and opened the wax paper that covered his.

"It's great," she said past her food, then swallowed. "So you do this every Sunday?"

"As many as possible."

They ate in silence for a few minutes. Avery watched the horses graze as she munched, and when she looked back at Hank, she caught him watching her.

"What?" she asked, licking her fingers.

"You're beautiful." He passed her a muffin. "That's all."

"Oh…" Coming from him it sounded more like a confession than a compliment. "Are you still my boss after hours?"

"Yep." He grinned.

"So this is really unprofessional, then," she teased.

"Entirely. Mr. Harmon would have a word with me if he saw this." But there was humor in his eyes. "Seriously, though, I promised myself I'd keep on the proper side of that line with you. So that's what I'm going to do."

She found herself feeling a little disappointed in that, and a little thrilled that he'd even had to make that promise. He was older, wiser, rugged—and definitely tempting. It was a rush to realize that she tempted him, too. They both knew how things stood—but out here in the rippling grass, horses grazing a few yards off, it felt like the rules no longer applied.

Although of course they did, she reminded herself firmly.

"I was surprised," she said after a moment. "All of the other ranch hands have been really…" Distanced. Nervous. Eerily formal. "…polite since I've arrived."

"Oh, that." He didn't say anything more.

"What?" she pressed. "I'm used to more chitchat, and you'd think I was a nun."

"I threatened them with bodily harm if I saw them

treating you with anything less than respect," he replied, a quirky smile coming to his lips. "And they believed me."

"So that was you?" she asked. Somehow she'd suspected as much.

"Yeah… I thought it would make life easier for you."

He'd been looking out for her from the beginning. It was sweet, actually. She'd expected to have to bend back a few fingers or knee a groin or two, but none of that had been necessary.

"You're a very sweet man, Hank."

"You think?" Color tinged his face. Had she actually made him blush?

"You are," she confirmed. "I'm used to something different with men."

Or maybe it was just the men she had dated. So far, she'd never met a man quite like Hank.

"You should get used to something better," he said. "Because I'm just doing the bare minimum here."

She lifted the half-finished muffin. "Are you sure?"

"Alright, I'm going a tad further than usual," he said, the humorous gleam coming back to his eye. "But everything else is on par with other employees. I often hold the hand of a cowboy to make sure he doesn't twist his ankle in the dark."

Avery laughed. "Do you now?"

"Several times a week." The smile faded, and he rose to his feet. "Come here."

He held out his hand and she took it, allowing him to pull her up. He didn't let go, instead leading her up the swell of a nearby hill. She was breathing hard by the time they crested it to look down over a cow-dotted plain. A tree-lined creek meandered away from the craggy blue mountains in the distance, and the low of cattle reached them on the breeze like Nature's own lullaby.

"That's where we work," Hank said, close to her ear. "Just you and the cattle…sometimes another guy on a horse when it takes more than one, but most times, just you."

"Isn't it lonely?"

"Yeah, can be." His voice was soft, and when she looked at him, he brushed a stray tendril off her forehead. "A guy gets a lot of time to think out there. Mull stuff over. Make his peace with whatever eats away at him."

"Like what?"

"Gotta say, Avery, the last little while, all I've been thinking about is you."

His gaze moved over her face, and down to her mouth. His lips parted, and she could feel the tension in his stance. He leaned closer, then stopped.

"Are you going to kiss me?" she whispered.

"Promised I wouldn't…" But his eyes were still fixed on her mouth, and when she leaned toward him ever so little he let out a soft moan. "I promised myself, Avery…"

It was rare to feel like the one in control with this rugged cowboy, and she realized with a rush that she liked it. He'd promised himself to behave, but she hadn't. She leaned closer still, and tipped her face up toward his. She could see what he wanted by the glitter in his eyes, but he still didn't make a move.

"Are you sure?" she asked with a teasing smile.

"Yup." But he didn't step back.

She put her hands on his biceps, stood up onto the tips of her toes, then let her eyes flutter shut as she touched her lips ever so gently to his.

That was all it took for his hands to slide around her waist and pull her hard against him. He responded to her as he took control of the kiss. His hand moved up her spine, then plunged into her hair. Her breath quickened and her heart pounded in her ears. She realized that she wasn't exactly prepared for this—she didn't know how to respond to this level of desire—but she wanted to. He seemed to know exactly what he was doing, and she felt the warmth of his work-roughened hand move underneath her shirt and over the bare skin of her waist.

She should stop…she knew that. This was quickly going further than she'd intended, and he seemed to have a lot more experience in these things than she did. She put her hands on his chest and pushed herself back.

Hank released her, closed his eyes and heaved a guttural sigh. "Sorry."

"I just…" She touched her hands to her warm cheeks. She hadn't meant to start that, exactly. Although, she should have known better than to toy with a man who had a decade more experience than she did.

"I don't do casual very well," she admitted. "I've tried it before, and my heart always gets trampled. So I know better… I shouldn't have started that."

"I don't do casual very well, either." He smiled uncertainly. "You're right. Doing this now…it's a bad idea. You've got a life in Kansas, and I've got one here. And frankly, if anyone were to see us, I could find myself out of work."

She still felt breathless; her knees were slightly weak. She knew what she wanted, and it was to see what happened next—if she didn't stop him...

"We should get back," she said instead.

He scooped up her hand in his warm grip and they walked down the hill toward the horses. That one had been her fault—she'd been the one to push past the line. She wasn't sorry that she'd done it...not exactly. She felt a little foolish, though, for not anticipating how he'd react. A chaste little peck on his lips wasn't going to stay chaste.

"Avery..."

She looked up at him and found those blue eyes fixed on her.

"I'll never push you into anything," he said. "I don't want you to feel nervous about being alone with me. I'm not the kind of guy who would take advantage. You're safe with me...okay?"

Safe. That was exactly how she felt with this cowboy. But this was short-term, and she had no business getting attached, because when her heart inevitably got broken, there was no one left to catch her when she fell.

THAT EVENING, HANK finished his rounds and headed back to the main house to drop off some paperwork. His mind was still on the feeling of Avery's lips. That woman could stir up his blood like no other!

She'd been the one to kiss him, and all that self-control had evaporated when her lips touched his. At first, he'd meant to kiss her back just as sweetly, but that lasted for all of a second before his instincts took over and that burn deep inside him ignited. He'd wanted to taste her, to pull her into him, to feel her against him with so much desire that it had taken every ounce of his willpower to release her when she'd pulled back. Not even Vickie had done that to him—not like this—and it scared him a little. He'd been married for twelve years, but other than Vickie, he didn't have a lot of experience. This was how hearts got mangled, and his was just as vulnerable as Avery's right now.

Hank had told himself he wouldn't kiss Avery again, and he'd meant it. He wasn't the kind of guy who toyed with a woman's emotions, and she was young. The age difference seemed to disappear when he was with her, but that didn't change the fact that he already had a marriage and a divorce under his belt. He'd seen more than she had, and he couldn't take advantage of that. He also had more to lose than she did.

He was a man who'd worked for everything he'd ever gotten. His pride depended on that, and getting fired? His pride wouldn't survive that, either. He refused to go hat in hand to his cousin Chet to ask for a job. Chet had his brother, Andy, to manage his ranch, which meant that the only positions available would be as ranch hand, and he didn't want to go back to that. This might be a vacation flirtation for her, but his whole life could be torn apart.

Hank parked his truck next to Mr. Harmon's black Ford and hopped out. Clouds were closing in, and Hank paused to look at the gathering storm. They'd have rain tonight—there was no doubt of that. At least it had been sunny for his afternoon ride. He'd crossed lines, but he didn't regret it. He'd just have to make sure he didn't do it again—his famous last words, it seemed.

"Evening, Hank," Mr. Harmon said as Hank let himself in the side door. The older man sat at the table, a ledger open in front of him as he went down the columns with a pencil in hand.

Hank dropped his paperwork into a file folder. "Evening, boss."

"How was your day?" Mr. Harmon asked, glancing up, but his gaze was a little more direct than the casual words suggested.

"Fine," Hank said. "You?"

His boss shrugged. "Not too bad."

"Avery—the new cook—wanted to speak with you tomorrow morning."

Mr. Harmon looked up, his expression guarded. "About?"

"You'd have to ask her."

Hank sure wasn't going to get into the middle of that.

"Alright," Mr. Harmon said with a nod. "And speaking of the cook, I've heard something, and I wanted to ask you about it."

Owen had spilled it to his father; Hank could feel it. Anxiety wormed up inside of him—what would he say? What *could* he say? He sighed, then nodded. "Sure. What's going on?"

"You know my stance on workplace relationships," his boss said.

"Clear as day, sir."

"So, you wouldn't be starting something up with our new cook, would you?"

Hank shut his eyes for a moment, gathering his own calm. It might not have been Owen. It could have been any other ranch hand who'd seen all the time he'd been spending with her lately, or noticed some passing glance between them. Whatever had grown between him and Avery hadn't been planned, but it was there nonetheless.

"Sir, I wouldn't jeopardize my position here by flagrantly breaking a rule. I'll admit that I'm attracted to her, but I have my priorities straight. You have nothing to worry about from me."

Mr. Harmon regarded him for a moment, then nodded. "I'll take your word on that. I'd hate to lose you, Hank. You're the best manager I've ever had, but I'm a man of my word, too. And fair is fair on this ranch. What's good for the ranch hand is good for the manager."

"I hear you, sir."

Hank finished putting away a few forms, desperate to get out of there. What exactly had his boss heard? What had been seen? If someone had come across them in the field... He grimaced, then turned for the door.

"Good night, sir. See you in the morning."

"Good night."

She was the one who kissed me. But that didn't matter, because Louis was looking to Hank for professionalism and self-control.

And when he crawled into bed that night, he listened to the rain coming down in a steady downpour, drenching fields and filling streams. They needed this. Montana summers tended to be hot and dry, so they counted on the storms for much-needed moisture. It was only June and they hadn't seen the real heat yet, but any ranching man knew what was coming. If only he'd been a little better at foreseeing the complications from their pretty cook.

Hank had stayed up later than usual tonight, his mind still spinning from the day's events, and by the time his head hit the pillow, the rain that normally soothed him only kept him awake. He couldn't get Avery out of his mind...not that he was trying all that hard.

His spare, pristine house that had no record of a woman left in it felt slightly empty. Would it be so terrible to have a woman's hairbrush on the counter in his bathroom, or the scent of body lotion or perfume lingering on the other pillow? Except he wasn't imagining just any woman; in his mind's eye, it was Avery with those red curls splayed across the pillow as she smiled over at him...

That wasn't helping matters. It only made him think of things he couldn't have. Neither of them were the "casual" kind, and even if they were, he'd be fired for it. That had been a warning if he'd ever heard one.

He'd been lying in bed for two hours already and sleep was still eluding him. He'd been happy with his life up until that slim redhead arrived on Harmon Ranch. He'd been intrigued by her from the beginning, first because he was suspicious of her motives, but the boundaries had gotten blurred somehow. It was nothing more than attraction, right? He'd known her for barely two weeks, and she was on her way out of town... She was telling Mr. Harmon who she was tomorrow, and what would happen then? This playacting of hers, pretending to be a cook when she really wanted to get to know her dad, would be over.

Hank pushed back his sheet and swung his legs over the side of the bed. Outside, the wind howled and the rain had gone from a patter against the glass to a drumroll. This was turning into a much wilder storm than the weather forecast had anticipated. He went to the window and shaded his eyes to look out. Tree branches whipped back and forth in the roiling wind and he heard a crack and a boom as lightning lit up the night sky. Tonight it was storming, and tomorrow all would be still...

This was how life worked. Storms could pass. Passion could simmer back down again. If he waited long enough, he could return to his regular routine and forget about whatever had him so fixated on Avery. Would Mr. Harmon be happy at the news? Would Avery's connection to this place be at an end? It might very well be that an introduction would be enough for her, at least for the next few years. She'd been raised by her mother and hadn't even known her father's name, after all. One thing was certain, when she spoke with Mr. Harmon the next day, everything would change. And that certainty put an ache into the center of his chest.

Hank turned on the TV, which was already on the weather channel. The banner at the bottom of the screen announced high wind warnings for their county. Yeah, that was obvious. The wind buffeted the house with hammering rain. He should probably take a quick look around the main buildings to make sure everything was okay.

He sighed and looked around for his jeans. His cell phone rang and he snatched it up from his bedside table.

For a split second he wondered if it would be Avery, but when he looked at the number, it was his boss. He felt a snag of disappointment.

"Hello, sir," Hank said, picking up. "Everything okay?"

"Hank, the wind is bad out there—have you been out?"

"Just on my way to do a check, sir."

"I can save you the time. I just got back and it's shaken loose the shingles on the hay barn roof. Peeled them right back and they flew off. We've got rain pouring in there!"

That would mean that their store of dry hay was getting drenched. Wet hay would rot, and their hay stock would be useless. This was an emergency.

"I'm on it, boss," Hank said, grabbing his jeans as he spoke. "I'll wake up the guys and we'll get to work."

"Thanks, Hank."

Hank didn't wait for a goodbye, but hung up and shoved his feet into the legs of his jeans. There was no time to waste. With all the ranch hands working together, they'd still be at this for most of the night. But that was part of the job on a ranch.

Five minutes later and fully dressed, Hank plunged into the storm. A rain slicker and his hat would have kept him dry if it weren't for the howling, driving wind. Thunder rumbled and there was another crack of lightning. It was going to get worse before it got better.

He jumped into his truck and turned the key. As the engine rumbled to life, his mind was already shooting ahead to the job. He needed two teams—one covering the exposed hay with tarps, and the other working on a patch for the roof. They could fix it properly after the storm passed. The men would be working hard for several hours, and they'd be hungry, which meant they needed Avery in the kitchen whipping up some snacks and hot coffee to keep them going.

The storm had turned the gravel road into mud, and as his tires hit a pothole, the whole vehicle lurched. His wipers whipped back and forth, and he could see the heaving, bending trees in the beams of his headlights.

The cows would be all right. They'd press together for warmth and safety, find some shelter in the tree lines. It was the hay that worried him, and the barn that housed the sick and injured animals. Those were the top priority.

When he arrived at the bunkhouse, he parked as close as he could to the front door. The wind blew the door hard against him and he grunted with the effort of just getting out of his truck. Rain whipped straight past the brim of his hat and into his face. By the end of this night, he'd be drenched to the bone. He pulled open the bunkhouse's front door and let it bang shut behind him. It was warm inside, and he could hear the rain pounding on the roof overhead.

"Rise and shine, gentlemen!" he called. "It's a bad storm, and we're on duty!"

He knocked sharply on every door he passed, and he could hear the moans, curses and rustle of men rousing themselves for a night of work. Avery's door was at the end of the hall, and he paused in front of it for a moment before knocking.

"Avery?" he called. He didn't hear a response, and he knocked again. "Avery?"

There was the sound of movement, then the chain

lock scraped and the door opened. Avery stood there in a nightgown. It was simple—a cotton T-shirt-style garment that ended at her knees. Her hair was tangled and she blinked at him blearily.

"Hank?" His name in her sleepy voice made him want things that he had no right to, and that he certainly didn't have time for. He glanced irritably down the hallway. Men were emerging from their rooms, hopping on one foot as they pulled on socks. A couple of ranch hands were looking at him in curiosity. The last thing he needed was to have more gossip flying around…

"There's a bad storm," he said, turning his attention back to the bleary-eyed woman before him. "We've got to go patch a roof, so we'll need food and hot drinks for the men when they come for a break."

"Oh…" She was waking up now, and she nodded, licked her lips. "So sandwiches, maybe? Muffins? Coffee?"

"Perfect," he said. "We need you to start right away, and I'll get the guys organized."

"Okay." She pushed her hair away from her forehead. "I'll just get dressed."

He wanted to kiss her again, even if only on her forehead. He wanted to pull her against him, feel the warmth of her face through his shirt. He wanted to tell her how pretty she looked when she was all foggy from sleep… "Thanks," he said instead and headed back down the hallway.

"Alright, guys," he said, raising his voice. "I need two teams…"

The night was only beginning.

Chapter Twelve

It was nearly one o'clock in the morning when Avery brought the coffee carafes into the dining room. She had made two platters of sandwiches. That likely wouldn't be enough, but it was a start. She'd pulled a large plastic bag filled with muffins out of the deep freeze and put them in a warm oven to thaw. They were still a little frozen in the centers and rather warm on the outsides, but they'd be edible, and the men wouldn't be complaining at this time of night. The creamers were full, as were the sugar dispensers.

She stood alone amongst the tables, listening to the storm crashing outside. Hank was out there somewhere, and she wished she knew where. That wasn't her business, though, was it? He wasn't her concern—and if she tried to make him her business, she could get him fired. What they had was some strange attraction, a connection like she'd never experienced before, but it wasn't enough. Hank had a lot more life experience than she did, so maybe there was a name for this... Star-crossed? But still, she wanted him to be safe.

"He knows what he's doing," she muttered to herself. He'd been working a ranch for over a decade, so she wasn't exactly going to rescue him from work he knew like the back of his hand.

When he was nineteen and started out as a ranch hand, she'd been helping her mother in the flower shop. She used to cut stems and make simple arrangements. Her mother used to praise her for having *the eye of an artist*. And now, as she stood here knowing that she was in over her head with Hank, that she couldn't pull herself out unscathed, she missed that store so desperately that it brought a lump to her throat.

In Winona's Wilderness, there had always been answers and explanations. In that shop, she'd been adored and treated like she was the most important person in her mother's life.

I can't leave you much, sweetheart, her mother used to tell her, *but I'll leave you a thriving business. A woman needs to be able to provide for herself if she's going to make her own rules. And, Avery...* Her mother would look her in the eye at this point. *Trust me. You're going to want to make your own rules.*

Avery spun her bracelet on her wrist, looking down at the words etched across the front: *Home is where the heart is.* That little flower shop on the corner of a street in a medium-sized town in Kansas had been filled to the brim and overflowing with heart.

She needed to go home. She'd come here for a reason—to meet her father—and while she didn't intend to leave without telling him who she was, she desperately wanted to get back home, where she knew who she was. She could worry about flower orders and deliveries. Instead of being in a drafty canteen, she'd be in her cozy apartment above the flower shop where rain would just be rain, drumming on the windows and making the indoors that much more snug.

What would her mother have told her about Hank, had she been here? Avery could hear her mother's voice. *He told you from the start that he didn't want more, dear. You have to believe people when they tell you who they are. I'm sorry he hurt you, but you can't say he wasn't honest.*

The front door opened and a rush of cold, wet air flooded inside followed by the broad shoulders of a man in a rain slicker. When he lifted his head, she recognized Louis.

"Mr. Harmon," she said. "I've got some refreshments out if you're hungry."

"No, no..." Louis shook off his coat. "That's not for me, that's for the boys. Just came to check on you. Everything okay?"

"Yes, fine." She nodded and stepped away from the table so that he could see the waiting food. Louis crossed the room and stood next to her, surveying her hard work. The front door opened and a couple of ranch hands came inside and beelined toward the food.

"Nicely done." He nodded, and they moved farther across the room, giving the men some space to eat. "Not bad for being hauled out of your bed at midnight."

She smiled tiredly. "I was fine once I woke up all the way."

Louis nodded again, and he looked at his boots but

didn't speak for a couple of beats. Then he looked over at her. "So you saw Chris Mayfield?"

"Yes, I did." Avery pulled a hand through her hair. "And Hillary confirmed all that when I saw her at the school."

The door banged shut again as two more men came inside, shaking their wet hats off as they headed toward the food.

"Hank told me that you wanted to speak with me," he said, "but I wanted to talk to you, as well. Maybe somewhere more private? It's going to be busy in here."

Avery followed Louis into the kitchen and they let the door swing shut behind them, muffling some of the noise outside.

"I mentioned to Hank that I wanted you to see Chris Mayfield because…" Louis paused, huffed out a breath, then looked toward her cautiously. "Do you know who your father is, Avery?"

"Yes," she replied. But the question was, did he?

Louis brightened. "That's really good. I wasn't sure if your mother told you or not."

Her heart clenched in her chest and she stared at him, looking for some sort of emotional reaction from the man. *He knew?* So was he just generally indifferent?

"She didn't tell me for a long time," Avery said hollowly, and apparently this was why. Louis had room in his heart for his legitimate children, but not for her.

"I didn't put it together at first," Louis said. "I mean, your hair is a lot lighter than his, and you don't look much like the Mayfields, but—"

He thought… She almost laughed. "Chris Mayfield isn't my father."

Louis stopped, blinked. "He isn't?"

"No." She took a wavering breath. "You are."

Louis regarded her in silence for a moment, then shook his head. "No, I'm not."

Avery hadn't expected him to refute her that quickly. "She told me on her deathbed," she said, softening her tone. Why was she trying to lighten the blow here? "I know this is probably a shock, but she told me very clearly that my father was Louis Harmon."

Louis licked his lips, then pressed them together.

"And before you tell me that she might have made it up, my mom was a deeply religious woman. She wouldn't have chosen that moment to lie to me. If she didn't want me to know who my father was, she could have just as easily not said a word. She named you, Mr. Harmon."

"Perhaps she was thinking of the one night we spent together…" Louis smiled wistfully. "She must have taken pity on a dorky kid, because she was gorgeous and I was all elbows and knees."

"But you did share something," she prodded.

"Yes." He nodded. "Once. She'd broken up with Chris Mayfield for the fifth or sixth time, and she was sad, and I cared. One thing led to another, and…" He spread his hands. "But it never happened again. It was our secret."

"Well, your secret made me," Avery said with a shrug. "I hate to break it to you."

"The red hair?" he asked.

"I don't know. Genetics can be weird. I'm sure there's a redhead somewhere in my family."

He didn't want to believe this, and while she'd known that she wouldn't be good news, exactly, this was worse than she'd imagined it. It wasn't right that a woman had to argue her own father into acknowledging her.

"I know you have a family," Avery began. "I know you have kids and you'll want to protect them. I'm not asking for anything. I don't need money—my mother left me an inheritance including her flower shop. All I wanted was…" Tears misted her eyes. "I wanted you to know that I existed."

"Oh, dear girl…" Louis reached out and squeezed her hand. "I would be more than honored to claim you as my daughter if it were true. You're beautiful, kind, persistent—and I'd be so very proud. It isn't that. I can't possibly by your father, Avery."

"That one night—" Did she really have to give him a biology lesson? "It was enough, you know."

"I'm sterile."

Avery blinked. "What?"

"I got mumps as a young teenager and it left me sterile. I can't produce children. It's a secret that I've kept for a long time because I didn't want my children to know."

"Owen and Olivia…" Her voice shook. "They aren't yours?"

"Carla and I had a rough patch and she left me for about six months. She came back pregnant with twins." Louis swallowed hard. "I had a choice. Send her packing and try to move on with someone else, or accept her back, babies and all. I loved her too much, and I told her that we'd raise those children together. Everyone in Hope assumed that we'd finally gotten pregnant after we reconciled, and that's the story we put out there. But my kids aren't mine...biologically."

"Oh..." Avery swallowed hard, her mind spinning as she processed this new information.

"I'm not your father, Avery. It isn't possible. I'm sorry."

There was a rustle behind them. They'd been angled away from the door—some semblance of privacy, perhaps—and Avery turned to see Owen through the window in the swinging kitchen door. It was open a crack, and Owen's anguished gaze was fixed on his father. He slowly shook his head.

"Owen!" Louis started forward and hauled open the door.

"You aren't my dad?" Owen's lips trembled. "Seriously? You aren't my *father*?"

The rumble of ranch hands' voices broke off into a jagged silence in the other room. They had an audience.

"Of course I am!" Louis said, his voice suddenly too loud for the space. "Owen, come here."

"You just told her—"

"And that was true," his father replied, his tone growing firmer. "All of it is true. But your mother put my name on that birth certificate, and no one can tell me that you aren't my son. I raised you. I love you—"

"And you lied to me!" Owen looked around the kitchen in one frantic sweep and took a step back into the canteen. All of this was wrong... Louis wasn't her father—and she'd just forced a family secret out into the open. This was all her fault.

"Just leave me alone!" Owen said, tears welling up

in his eyes, then he turned and wove past the tables toward the door. Avery and Louis followed. Owen shoved
open the door, nearly colliding with Hank on his way
in, then the boy disappeared out into the storm. Everyone stood there immobile for a beat, but Avery knew
what she had to do... She had to fix this somehow.
She'd caused it.

"I'm going after him," she said, tightening her sweater
around her and heading out into the canteen. Every eye
was pinned to her as she wove through the same tables
that Owen had.

"Avery." Hank put a hand out to stop her. "What's
going on?"

But she didn't have time to explain. She needed to
talk to Owen and fix this if she could. She shot Hank
a look of apology, then ducked her head against the
downpour and dove out into the rain.

HANK LOOKED AT Mr. Harmon, confused. His boss
crossed the room and the cowboys all dropped their
gazes. What had just happened in here? All he'd seen
was Owen storming out, just about in tears, and Avery
dashing after him. He shook rain droplets off his sodden hat.

"What's going on?" he asked.

"She thought I was her father," he said, sounding a
little stunned. "I'm not."

The other ranch hands stared at each other mutely,
then headed for the door. That was the right call in Hank's
opinion. This was family business, and they had a barn
roof to patch.

Hank looked back at the door. Avery was already out there in the pounding rain. Another peal of thunder rumbled overhead. She shouldn't be out there running around in a storm. Owen was probably headed to the barn or somewhere relatively safe. She didn't have any protection from the elements.

"Owen will be fine," Mr. Harmon said, as if reading his mind. "But that girl shouldn't be running around in a storm. We're liable if she hurts herself."

"I'll go find her," Hank said. His boss nodded. Although he had a point, it wasn't about the dangers of a storm. She'd just found out that Mr. Harmon wasn't her dad, and he knew what that would do to her. Hank pushed open the door and headed out into the rain.

Owen was out of sight but Avery stood in the pouring rain clutching her sweater around her thin shoulders. Her hair was slicked to her head and hung in sodden ringlets down her back.

"Avery!" he called. She turned, her face as pale as moonlight in the darkness.

"I don't know where he went!" she shouted back.

Hank jogged across the muddy ground and stripped off his slicker, settling it around her trembling shoulders. "What's going on?"

"I told Louis...and..." She swallowed, looked over her shoulder again. "He's not my father, to start with, but it's more complicated than that. Owen heard it all. And I don't know where he's gone."

"He'll be fine," Hank said. "I know that kid. He's probably at the barn by now."

Tears mingled with the rain on her cheeks. "This is my fault."

"What's going on? I don't get it. How do you know that Mr. Harmon isn't your dad?" he asked, shaking his head.

"Because he isn't the twins' father, either. He's sterile."

"Wait…" Hank struggled to make sense of it all. "What?"

She explained the situation and when she was done, Hank was stunned. He'd had no idea.

"Come back inside," Hank said.

She shook her head. "No. Hank, I can't stay. I've caused enough trouble as it is—"

"So you're just leaving?" he demanded. "Just like that?"

"What would you have me do?" He'd known she was going, but not like this—not with two minutes to put together everything he wanted to say to her before it was over. She didn't need to do anything…He wasn't asking anything of her except—

He glanced over his shoulder. He could see Louis standing in the doorway watching them.

"Stay!" Hank pleaded.

"I just caused a major family rift in there!" She jutted a finger toward the canteen. "I'm not going to be welcome, Hank! I've said my piece, I've discovered that my mom was wrong and I need to go. That was the plan."

"Screw the plan," he growled. "Stay with me."

"You know I can't." Her lips quivered with repressed

emotion. "If it were just you and me…but it isn't. And everything is so much more complicated—"

"Damn it, Avery, I love you!" He hadn't meant to say it—hadn't even realized what all of these jarring emotions meant until the words tore out of him.

She stared at him in stunned silence for a few beats. "You do?" she stammered.

It was a strange relief to just admit it. Denying his feelings hurt more.

"Yes. Don't just walk away. Give us a chance."

Avery wiped at her face with the tips of her fingers— all that showed from under his slicker.

"My mother would have warned me away from you," she said with tears in her voice.

"Do you feel it, though?" he asked, pulling her closer. "Or is this completely one-sided? I need to know."

"I love you, too." Her voice was so quiet that he almost didn't catch her words. He knew that Mr. Harmon was watching them, but he didn't care anymore. He pulled her against him and caught her lips with his. She loved him… That was more than he'd even dared to hope right now.

When he finally pulled back, he said, "Please stay. We'll figure something out."

"Hank, we don't have a future," she said, shaking her head. "I'm going back to Kansas. Why don't you come with me?"

That was a lot to ask. He couldn't just relocate to a new state and seriously date this woman without a steady income. Yet he was asking her to do the same thing, wasn't he? He looked toward the canteen again.

Louis was no longer in the doorway, but he must have seen enough. Hank had just lost his job.

"I can get another job here," he said. "I have family. There's got to be a Granger somewhere who will hire me. I'm not saying it'll pay well, but it'll be something."

"It isn't the money, you lout." Tears sparkled in her eyes. "You can't give me what I want here, either, Hank. I want to get married. Maybe not today, or tomorrow, but I do want marriage…"

He could feel the futility of it all rising up inside him. He'd known he should have kept his distance, but he hadn't heeded reason. And now he'd gone and crossed all those lines—kissed her in front of his boss. He'd just thrown it all away for Avery, and it couldn't work between them.

"I've been married before," he said. "You know I can't do it again."

"I know," she said, her gaze meeting his sadly. "I have to go back to Kansas to reopen my mother's store. It's home, Hank. I have to go *home*."

Home. He understood that. This place had been his home, too, and he wanted her to continue fitting in here in Hope… He wanted more rides with her, more walks, more chances to eat her awful cooking. He wanted to cook for her, too—wake her up to omelets and waffles…whip up a Sunday afternoon pot of creamy soup to share… But he couldn't offer what she needed. He was bitter and broken, and he couldn't blame her for refusing to settle for less.

"So is this it?" he asked, a lump in his throat nearly choking off his words. "Is this goodbye?"

She nodded. "I'll leave in the morning. I think Louis will understand if I don't give notice."

Hank pulled her into his arms once more and held her close. He leaned his cheek against her wet hair and inhaled the scent of her.

"If you ever change your mind…" he said, but he knew better. She was her mother's daughter, and when Winona had walked away from this town, it had been for good. Avery was going home where she belonged, and he had to let her.

Hank released her, and she shrugged out of his jacket and handed it back. She hunched her shoulders against the rain and headed toward the bunkhouse, and he stood there with his slicker in one hand, forcing himself to stay put. Because if he took one step, it was going to be to run after her, and that was pointless.

He'd known it from the start.

Chapter Thirteen

Avery turned off the water, then dropped her robe and stepped into the bathtub. She was cold and wet to the skin from the rain, and the warm water enveloping her was a welcome comfort. She leaned her head against the wall and shut her eyes.

She was exhausted. It was almost two in the morning, and had she stayed in Kansas where she belonged, she'd be fast asleep right now. Coming to Hope in search of her father had been foolish. What made her think that her mother had been wrong to hide her past? Winona had never done anything without a good reason, so why did Avery have to question that after her death?

Except Avery knew her curiosity would never have allowed her to let this be. Her mother gave her the name of her biological father...or at least the name of the man she thought was Avery's father. She'd tried.

"Mom, you died too soon..." she whispered, tears slipping past her lashes. She still needed her mother. Even at the age of twenty-four she needed mothering. Would that ever go away, that longing to be someone's child? Perhaps that was why she'd come out here—to be someone's child again.

Now, though, Avery wished that she'd never come. Her mother was not going to be replaced by a dad who was a stranger. She could see why her mother had wanted Louis to be the man. Louis was gruff and sweet, everything she'd have wanted in a father. Unfortunately, he wasn't hers...

It was possible that Chris Mayfield was her dad, but did she want to do this all over again—thrust herself into the middle of someone else's family? Not really... This experience with the Harmons had given her a hearty dose of reality. No matter how good the man, she'd be a shock. And with her mother's early tendency to look for love in all the wrong places, as Louis put it, Pastor Mayfield might not be her father, either...

No, she was done looking for her dad. If she ever changed her mind, she'd approach it differently, but she might never be ready to try again.

Hank had been the warm spot in this debacle. The memory of the way his lips felt against hers still made her tingle, even through her sadness. Avery would never forget Hank. She'd accidentally fallen in love with him, and while she knew they had no future, the thought of leaving him behind still felt like a piece of her was being carved out of her chest.

She rubbed her hands over her face, sniffling back the tears.

And he loves me, too... That made it worse. It would be easier if her feelings weren't reciprocated and he felt nothing for her but friendship. Then she could snap herself out of this… She'd always been practical, but his kisses, the way his arms slid around her and held her so securely…those were memories she couldn't banish.

After she warmed up in the tub, she let out the water and got back into her bathrobe. She stood in the center of the bedroom for a long while, then went to her bag and pulled out a pad of paper and a pen. She propped up some pillows against the headboard of her bed and crawled on top of the quilt.

She was leaving in the morning after she put out the cereal for breakfast. There was no reason why the men should go hungry. She'd do her job for the last time, and then she'd go back where she belonged.

Dear Louis,
I apologize for the pain I've put your family through. I had no intention of upsetting your children or revealing secrets. I had only wanted to meet my father, and I can see why my mother wanted so badly for you to be him.

You are a kind man and a fair boss. Your children are lucky to have you, and I wish you only happiness in the future.

Please forgive me for leaving without saying goodbye. I thought it would be better if I just went home. I'm not a very good cook, anyway. Just ask Hank. He's a good manager—you're lucky to have him running your ranch.
Avery Southerly

She tore off the sheet and folded it. She'd leave it on her bed to be found after she left in the morning. She'd miss Louis, she realized. He wasn't her father, but he might be the closest she'd get to meeting a father of her own. If she'd have been able to conjure up a father out of ideals and hopes, Louis would have been the result. He was a good man, and her mother had obviously felt the same. Winona wasn't a liar. But she was a woman, and even she could fall victim to her own deepest wishes...

But Louis wasn't the only one she'd miss, and she'd left Hank's letter for last because it would be harder to write. She picked up the pad again, and wrote the first words: *Dear Hank.*

She stopped there, her heart so full that she felt like it would burst. She had no words to encompass what she felt. They'd already said all they could say to each other, except for a proper goodbye. But she didn't trust herself, because if her lips touched his again, she'd stop thinking rationally and do something she'd regret.

Hank was heartbreak. He awoke things in her that she'd never experienced before, but he wouldn't be the one she'd marry. And she couldn't settle for less... Her mother had made mighty sure of that.

She sat with the pen poised over the paper, wishing that something new would come to her, some stroke of illumination that would make sense of it all. Her mother would have been able to help her. She'd have some insight that would give clarity, explanation. If her mother were here, Avery wouldn't be alone in this, because if there was one thing that Winona understood best, it was men. And heartbreak. And moving on.

Avery dropped the pen as her shoulders shook with sobs. She loved him, and right now nothing hurt more.

HANK WAS OUT checking on the barn long before sunup. The patch on the roof seemed to have held, and the storm from the night before had moved on, leaving them with crimson-splashed clouds as the sun edged over the horizon.

Hank had gone to bed around three, and had managed to sleep until four, then he was up again. Ordinarily, an hour of sleep for the night would leave him grouchy and in need of a nap, but not this morning. He was irritable, but it wasn't from lack of sleep. It was because in the space of one night, he'd let go of his self-control and lost everything that mattered most to him—his job, his home here at Harmon Ranch and the woman he'd fallen in love with against all his better instincts.

He'd been thinking about Avery all night. He'd told himself that he'd wait until breakfast to talk to her, that maybe things would look different in the light of day. Maybe it would hurt less. Maybe it would seem more like the logical and necessary ending of a short fling. Except Avery was no fling. It might have been short, but he hadn't been toying with her. This wasn't just physical—it had slipped deeper than that, and he'd fallen headlong in love with her.

Hank slowed his truck as he approached the Harmon house. He squinted against the slanted rays of morning sunlight, shading his eyes with one hand. Had he seen that right?

Mr. Harmon was standing outside in his bathrobe and

slippers, waving frantically. Olivia was in the doorway, also in a bathrobe. Hank gunned the motor and took a sharp turn up the drive to the house. Something was wrong—something more than the fact that Mr. Harmon was going to fire him today. He unrolled his window.

"Boss?"

"Hank!" Louis came up to the side of the truck. "Have you seen Owen?"

"No. I was just at the barn, and he wasn't out there. Why? Didn't he come home last night?"

"Yes, he came back last night," Louis said. "He was in his room before I went to bed. But he was gone this morning."

Hank's stomach sank. The kid had been through a lot in the last few hours, but he wasn't the running away type. Still—

"Did he leave a note? Pack a bag?" Hank searched his mind for any information that might help. "I don't know... Are any of his clothes missing?"

"Not that I can tell." Louis rubbed a hand over his graying hair. "I tried talking to him last night about his mom and I... He wouldn't listen. I talked to Olivia and Owen together, but—"

The older man's eyes misted with tears.

"Mr. Harmon," Hank said. "I have an idea of where he might be. I'll go see if I can find him, okay?"

His boss nodded. "Thank you, Hank."

Apparently, losing his job would have to wait. Hank had been planning to head back to the canteen to see Avery, but that would have to wait, too. He couldn't leave Owen out there alone, not while it was possible he'd still do something stupid that would break his dad's heart. Owen was a good kid, but he was also sixteen, and things were more passionate at that age.

Hank put the truck into gear and drove straight through the Harmon property and up to the highway. If Owen was anywhere, it would be at his mother's grave—Hank was willing to bet on it. For Owen, this was all about his mom, so that was where he'd go for his answers.

As Hank sped along the highway toward town, the sun rose slowly into the sky, bathing the land in a rosy, golden haze. The fields stretched out on either side of the road, making him feel small in comparison to it all, but his heart was still heavy. He already missed Avery like an ache in the center of him. They'd said it all last night—he knew that. He couldn't offer her anything more than what he already had, and he knew as well as she did that it wasn't enough. He wanted to put off the goodbye, but that wasn't fair to her. He did need to talk to her, though. Maybe he needed to hear it all again to hammer it home—he was a man, after all.

Hank took the turn onto the road that led up to the country church, and when he approached the building he saw one of the ranch trucks parked out front. He felt a wave of relief that his gut instinct had been right.

Hank parked his truck next to Owen's, and got out. The sun was slowly rising in the sky, dew sparkling on every blade of grass and glistening on the fence posts. Owen was crouched near the edge of the small grave-yard. He glanced back as Hank slammed his door shut, the boy's expression sullen.

"What?" Owen asked testily.

"You scared your dad," Hank said.

"I'm fine."

"Are you?" Hank squinted and Owen turned back to the gravestone. Their shadows were long in the early morning sunlight, and Hank sucked in a chestful of flower-scented air. He'd always loved this place—not the graveyard, exactly, but the church and the garden surrounding it. It was peaceful.

"Why didn't they tell me?" the boy asked after a few beats of silence.

"Probably because it embarrassed them," Hank replied with a shrug. "Nobody likes to share that kind of thing."

"He wasn't my dad…" Owen still sounded incredulous. "All this time, and I had no idea."

"He *is* your dad," Hank said.

"No, my mom and some other guy—" Owen turned back toward Hank. "Who *was* my real father?"

"I have no idea who your biological father is," Hank said. "But I know who your real dad is. He's the guy who held you when you were born and taught you how to walk. He's the guy frantically looking for you in his bathrobe now."

Owen heaved a sigh. "My sister already knew. Mom told her ages ago, and she kept it a secret."

That was actually a relief to Hank. He wasn't sure he could talk both twins down from the ledge on this one.

"They should have said something," Owen said, his voice thick.

"Yeah?" Hank asked. "You think so? Because I don't know how much your dad wanted to sit you down and tell you that your late mother had cheated on him. Those would be painful memories. He loved your mom something fierce, and when you love someone that much and they walk out—"

Emotion tightened Hank's voice, too, except it wasn't Vickie he was thinking about. It was Avery. She didn't want what he could offer… He could sympathize with his boss on that. When a woman a man loved that much didn't want what he could give, it gouged out a part of his heart that he didn't even know existed.

"Your parents would have wanted you to believe the best about them," Hank said at last. "I don't think there was any easy way to have that conversation."

Owen rubbed his hands over his eyes. "So who am I?"

"You're Owen Harmon. There's more than one way to make a family."

Owen was silent.

"Your mom and dad loved each other in a way that not everyone gets to experience," Hank went on slowly. "Everyone wants it, and everyone looks for it, but not everyone finds it. That doesn't mean they didn't hit some rough patches. Life can bc complicated sometimes, and at your age, you're not going to understand that. You probably think we adults are a bunch of idiots who mess up our lives out of sheer stupidity, but we don't…"

"Like Aunt Vickie?" Owen asked.

"Yeah, like Vickie." He sighed. And like Avery, too. "But when someone can get past the betrayal of an affair and love again, that's something uncommonly beautiful. Not many can do it, but your dad did. He loved her so much that he was willing to put aside the fact that you kids weren't biologically his and love you just as though you were. He wanted to keep you all together."

"You think it's the same for him?" Owen whispered.

"Yup."

The boy sucked in a deep breath. "I miss my mom."

"I know." Hank put a hand on his shoulder. "But you still have your dad, and right now he's worried sick about you."

"I should probably give him a call…" Owen looked over this mother's grave once more, then pulled his cell phone out of his pocket and turned it on.

Mr. Harmon needed to hear from his son personally. "Now, I'm going to give you some privacy here to talk to your dad, and I'm going to head back to the ranch."

"Okay." Owen nodded. "Thanks, Uncle Hank."

"You promise me that you're coming home," Hank added.

"Yeah, I'm coming home."

That would do. Hank turned and headed back to the truck, his heart still raw, but his mind was going over a new thought. He got back into his truck and turned the key, the engine coughing to life.

When Vickie had cheated on him, she'd broken his heart and his self-confidence all at once. She'd taken everything he had to offer—every last bit of him—and then handed it back all chewed up. He hadn't been good enough, and he'd never wanted to feel that kind of failure and rejection again. He'd never felt lower, never felt more worthless, and until this very moment, he'd never felt a deeper pain.

Well, Avery did love him, and her problem wasn't that he wasn't man enough or interesting enough... She wanted commitment. She wanted marriage, and he'd just spent the last five years being too afraid to try again.

He turned on the road that led to the highway. He'd thought that if he held back from committing, he'd save his heart, but that hadn't worked with Avery. It wasn't commitment that hurt so much when it came to her, it was the lack of it, the walking away. He wasn't going to just get over her. There'd be no forgetting that Avery had passed through his life, and if he let her leave, he'd never forgive himself, either.

He'd just told Owen that a man being able to get past the pain of an affair and love again was something uncommonly beautiful. Mr. Harmon had loved his wife again, and while Hank's heart wasn't ever going to return to Vickie, he had stumbled into loving again...

Avery wanted a husband, and there was no one he wanted to spend his life with more than that redhaired beauty. He'd be the man she needed, the man she wanted, and if she'd have him, he'd be hers till death parted them.

He had to talk to her. He stepped on the gas and his truck sailed on past the speed limit as he headed toward the ranch. He skidded to a stop in front of the canteen and threw himself out of the truck. It was empty, though, and when he poked his head through the swinging kitchen door, it was empty, too—the only sound that of a dripping tap. His heart sank, but it was possible she was in her room. He went back outside and jogged over to the bunkhouse.

The men were on their shifts with the cattle, and he headed down the hall to her room and knocked on the door.

Nothing.

He knocked again. "Avery?"

Still nothing. He tried the door, and it opened. Inside, the room was tidy, the bed made, her bags gone. In the center of the bed were two folded pieces of paper. He felt like the breath had been kicked out of him as he crossed the room and picked up the first. It was for Mr. Harmon and he set it aside. The second was for him.

Dear Hank...

He read it through, then shoved it into his pocket and headed back out to his truck. There was still the slightest chance that he could catch up with her, and he'd take those odds.

Chapter Fourteen

Avery was just approaching the town of Hope on the highway. She was driving in silence, unwilling to trust herself to listen to the radio in her current emotional state. She didn't need country music to remind her of what she didn't have. She didn't need heartbreaking melodies to crash through the thin veneer she was keeping up. Music was the answer when she could cry into her pillow, and not a minute before. The speed limit sign reminded her to check her speed, and she realized she'd been driving well under the speed limit already.

She had to pull herself together. At the very least she should to be able to drive the speed limit! She pulled a hand through her hair, waiting for that optimistic feeling of heading home to descend onto her. It always did when she was on her way back.

Except for this time. She blinked back a mist of tears.

"No," she said aloud. Crying while driving was a bad idea. She reached over and fiddled with her bracelet.

Home is where the heart is...

She was driving home... It was supposed to feel better than this. She was supposed to be leaving all of this behind her. She had Winona's Wilderness waiting. She had her apartment. Her friends. The customers who'd be so happy to have the store open once more.

Home had always been in Kansas, and she was reminded of Louis's lame joke about not being in Kansas anymore. But even Dorothy Gale had wanted to go back to Kansas after her adventure in Oz. *There's no place like home.* And she'd clicked her heels together three times to have her wish come true...

Except for some reason, Avery wasn't longing for Kansas. Her heart was still back on that ranch with a cowboy she had no business loving. Home had always been where her heart was—with her mom in that shop. But her mom was gone now, and while she'd thought that home would stay the same no matter what because of the memories there, was it possible that she was wrong?

A thump jarred her out of her reverie, and with every revolution of the tire, she heard a loud hiss.

A flat. Just her luck. She wasn't even in town yet where she could get to a mechanic. She sighed and pulled her car to the side of the road. Another truck sped on past, and Avery leaned her forehead against the steering wheel.

Her heart was now in Montana, and that wasn't a good thing. The man she loved didn't want what she did, even though he loved her. Life could be oh, so complicated...

She pulled out her cell phone. She'd have to call roadside assistance and have a tow truck sent her way. What was this highway called again? She looked out the windows but didn't see a road sign. Was this east of Hope, or west? Wait…north? She punched the GPS on her phone. There was no point calling anyone until she could tell them where she was.

An engine rumbled to a stop behind her, and she glanced in her rearview mirror but could only see grille. The truck's door opened, then banged shut, and she looked into her side mirror to see a familiar, lanky form jogging toward her car. Tears welled up in her eyes in spite of herself, and she undid her window.

"Hank," she breathed as he arrived at her door and leaned down. This wasn't going to make leaving any easier, but she was so glad to see him that she didn't care.

"Need a hand?" he asked, his voice low and warm.

"I have a flat tire." She pushed open the door and got out. She stood there looking at him in the morning light as vehicles whipped past them. Tears welled in her eyes, and he opened his arms.

"Come here," he said.

"I'm supposed to be leaving town," she said, swallowing a lump in her throat.

"Not going anywhere with a flat."

She stepped into his strong embrace and leaned her face against his chest. He smelled musky and safe, and she wished she could freeze time there on the cusp between going and staying, and never have to actually take the leap.

"What are you doing out here?" she asked, pulling back and looking up into his face.

"I was trying to catch up with you," he said. "I got this." He pulled her note to him out of his pocket, shook it open and began to read. "You said, 'My heart hurts writing this. I don't want to say goodbye, but I know it's for the best. I won't forget you—ever. Please don't forget me... If there is some small part of your heart that could hold onto me—'" His voice broke and he stopped, swallowed. "Avery, I've been doing some thinking."

He tucked the note back into his pocket and smoothed his hand over the side of her face. "Mr. Harmon did the impossible. He got over an affair and loved again— loved harder, loved stronger, loved deeper... Hard work seemed to work for them." He sucked in a breath. "I didn't think I could do that. I didn't think I could let myself go again. I thought I'd be able to protect myself if I didn't let myself fall in love, but then you came along..."

"I knew from the start that you didn't want that," she began. "And Louis will fire you—"

"No..." He shook his head. "I didn't want it. I was scared. But I fell in love with you anyway, and holding myself back isn't going to protect my heart at all. It's too late for that. As for getting fired..." He shrugged. "That's going to happen, anyway."

"So you missed me?" She smiled ever so slightly.

"You could say that..." He bent down and kissed her lips. "When I thought you'd gone and I'd never see you again, it hurt worse than I imagined possible. I love you, Avery. We might not have planned this, but it's a done deal. At least for me."

"What do you mean?"

Another car zoomed past, but his eyes didn't waver from hers. "I'm not going to just stop loving you. I'm not going to get bored of you. I'm not going to change my mind. I want to marry you, I want to have kids with you, I want grow old with you…if you'll have me."

Avery stared at him in shock. "You're asking me to marry you?"

"If you need to think about it, that's okay." He nodded quickly. "I kind of just dumped this on you. I get that. Why don't you come back with me. Stay a few days longer. Give me a chance to convince you."

Back to the ranch, to the family she'd wounded. She winced. "Louis isn't going to want to see me…" Louis might not want to see Hank again, either, for all she knew.

"You don't know him very well, then," he replied. "He's got a big heart, and things are patched up with the kids now. It'll be okay. If he still needs to let me go, I'll find something else. I'll tell you what—come back with me and give it a try, and if you don't feel like Montana can be home, then I'll go with you to Kansas."

"You'd do that for me?" Avery licked her lips, her heart beating wildly in her chest.

"I'd jump the moon for you, Avery." He looked down into her face, his eyes filled with pleading. "What do you say?"

"Yes." She nodded, and she wrapped her arms around his neck and stood up onto the tips of her toes to kiss him. He pulled her close and kissed her back quite thoroughly, and when he stopped, he gave her a peculiar look.

"Yes to which part?" he asked. "I kind of need to know…"

Avery's heart filled with love for this cowboy who'd somehow become her safe place. How had it happened, exactly, that this man had become Home?

"To all of it," she said. "I'll marry you, Hank, and I'll go back to the ranch with you, and if I hate it, I'll drag you back to Kansas with me."

"That's a deal," he said, and he lowered his lips over hers once more. He held her close to him, and she could feel the beat of his heart against her body. She wouldn't have been able to move if she tried, but she didn't want to move. She wanted to stay here in his arms for the rest of her life.

Her heart had finally come home.

Epilogue

In the little country church just outside of Hope, Montana, Avery stood in the foyer, fiddling with the edge of her veil. Up at the front of the church, Hank was standing there waiting for her, and the solemnity of the moment was just now settling onto her shoulders.

She was about to become Mrs. Avery Granger.

Pastor Mayfield was on vacation and another pastor from town was doing their ceremony. It was better that way. She still didn't know if Chris Mayfield was her father, but right now she didn't care. She'd found a family in the unlikeliest of places…the Harmon ranch.

Louis Harmon had just as big a heart as Hank had claimed, and he'd relented on his firing of Hank. He said that if they were getting married, who was he to rain on their parade? But more than that, Louis told her that he was honored to step in for her in an unofficial sort of way.

"Like an honorary dad," he'd said. "I think Winona would approve of that."

She had a feeling her mother would have approved of it, too. Winona had always wanted her daughter to have something better than she'd grown up with, and she'd managed that in every way possible. Even though the bracelet wasn't exactly wedding chic, she'd chosen to wear it on her special day as a way to keep her mother close.

Owen and Olivia had been glad to welcome her into the family. She was marrying Hank, and they liked her. Everyone liked her even more when Louis hired a real cook, and her services were no longer required. She went from cook to fiancée—and she'd been happy to set up the home she'd share with Hank. That place was so sterile, it was starved for a woman's touch.

Hank hadn't minded in the least as she added her own accents around the place. He said he was tired of sleeping spread eagle in the middle of a bed, and he couldn't wait to share it with her.

She still owned her mother's shop, but she'd hired a manager to run it for her, a single mother with a little girl. Avery would go back and check up on things every few weeks, but she was satisfied with how things were running so far. Winona's Wilderness would go on, and she hoped that the flower shop could be the saving grace of another mom and daughter.

And now she stood in this little church about to take the biggest step of her life, and her heart pattered in her chest. The organ music swelled—it was time. Louis patted her hand affectionately.

"Ready?" he asked with a smile.

"Ready."

And she was. She was readier for this than she'd been

for anything in her life. Marrying Hank was the home-coming she'd never known she'd needed.

The doors opened, and together they stepped into the aisle, her hand tucked into the crook of the arm of her stand-in dad. She looked up at Louis and he shot her a reassuring grin. Hank's eyes misted when he saw her, and her heart filled with love for the lanky cowboy who waited for her at the front of the church.

As she reached the front pew, Hank came down to meet her.

"Who gives this woman to be joined with this man in marriage?"

Avery's heart skipped a beat—the minister wasn't supposed to ask that question. He'd been told to leave that part out. It was awkward...difficult. Louis was standing in as father of the bride, but that question should be re-served for his daughter Olivia's wedding one day. Heat flooded Avery's cheeks, and her gaze whipped up to Louis, who didn't look the least bit fazed.

Louis smiled down at her proudly and his words re-verberated through the church. "Her mother and I do."

Avery blinked back fresh tears as she felt a wave of relief mingled with gratitude.

"You take good care of her, now," Louis murmured to Hank as he handed her over.

"It's a promise," Hank replied quietly, tucking Avery's hand into the crook of his own arm. He smiled down into her eyes, then they turned toward the minister.

They didn't have any history with this pastor, and he didn't know them very well, but it didn't matter. Their vows were for each other, and today, as they promised to love and support each other no matter what life threw in their direction, Avery didn't feel nervous in the least.

These vows were more than formality. They were the beginning of a home that would be the bedrock for their own children and grandchildren. Years later, her daughters would have her words echoing through their minds as they grew up and started their own families:

You come from a line of strong women. There were the Southerlys, and we stood strong no matter what. And you are a Granger, and we have character. Reputations can be tarnished, but reputations are only what other people think. I'm not concerned with other people's opinions. Your character—that's who you are at heart. You're a Granger, dearest, and we Grangers are nothing if not honest. We're tough, and we do the right thing. So you never forget who you are and where you came from.

* * * * *

Don't miss the next book in Patricia Johns's
HOPE, MONTANA *miniseries,*
coming in December 2017 from
Harlequin Western Romance.

And check out previous books in the miniseries:
HER STUBBORN COWBOY
THE COWBOY'S CHRISTMAS BRIDE
THE COWBOY'S VALENTINE BRIDE
THE TRIPLETS' COWBOY DADDY

Get 2 Free Books,

Plus 2 Free Gifts— just for trying the **Reader Service!**

HARLEQUIN® Western Romance

SPECIAL EXCERPT FROM

H HARLEQUIN®
™

ᴥWestern ᴿomance

Jason Till is the type of cowboy Sloane Hartley wants to avoid. But she can't seem to stop thinking about him...

Read on for a sneak preview of
HER TEXAS RODEO COWBOY,
part of Trish Milburn's
BLUE FALLS, TEXAS series!

By the time her mom rang the bell signaling lunch was ready, Sloane had learned that Jason was from Idaho, he'd been competing as a professional since he was eighteen and he'd had six broken bones thanks to his career choice.

"Are you eating with us?" Phoebe asked as she slipped her little hand into Jason's.

He smiled down at her. "I don't think they planned for the extra mouth to feed."

Sloane huffed at that. "You've never met my mother and her penchant for making twice as much food as needed."

"Please," Phoebe said.

"Well, how can I say no to such a nice invitation?"

Phoebe gave him a huge smile and shot off toward the picnic area.

Jason chuckled. "Sweet kids."

"Yeah. And resilient."

He gave her a questioning look.

"They come from tough backgrounds. All of them have had to face more than they should at their age."

"That's sad."

"It is. They seem to like you, though."

"And that annoys you."

"I didn't say that."

"You didn't have to." He grinned at her as he grabbed a ham-and-cheese sandwich and a couple of her mom's homemade oatmeal cookies.

"Sorry. I just don't know you, and these kids' safety is my responsibility."

"So this has nothing to do with the fact your sister is trying to set us up?"

"Well, there goes my hope that it was obvious only to me."

"It's not a bad idea. I'm a decent guy."

"Perhaps you are, but you're also going to be long gone by tomorrow night."

He nodded. "Fair enough."

Well, that reaction was unexpected. She'd thought he might try to encourage her to live a little, have some harmless fun. She wasn't a fuddy-duddy, but she also wasn't hot on the idea of being with a guy who'd no doubt been with several women before her and would be with several afterward.

Of course, she often doubted a serious relationship was for her either. She'd seen at a young age what loving someone too much could do to a person. The one time she'd believed she might have a future with a guy, she'd been proved wrong in a way that still stung years later.

Don't miss HER TEXAS RODEO COWBOY
by Trish Milburn, available September 2017
wherever Harlequin® Western Romance
books and ebooks are sold.

www.Harlequin.com

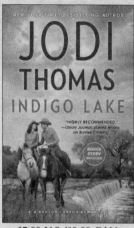

lover in you!

Earn points from all your Harlequin book purchases from wherever you shop.

Turn your points into *FREE BOOKS* of your choice
OR
EXCLUSIVE GIFTS from your favorite authors or series.

Join for FREE today at
www.HarlequinMyRewards.com.

Harlequin My Rewards is a free program (no fees) without any commitments or obligations.

MYR17

Looking for more satisfying love stories
with community and family at their core?

Check out **Harlequin® Special Edition**
and **Harlequin® Western Romance** books!

New books available every month!

CONNECT WITH US AT:

Harlequin.com/Community

Facebook.com/HarlequinBooks

Twitter.com/HarlequinBooks

Instagram.com/HarlequinBooks

Pinterest.com/HarlequinBooks

ReaderService.com

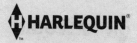

**ROMANCE WHEN
YOU NEED IT**

LOVE
Harlequin
romance?

Join our Harlequin community to share your
thoughts and connect with other
romance readers!

Be the first to find out about promotions,
news, and exclusive content!

Sign up for the Harlequin e-newsletter and
download a free book from any series at

www.TryHarlequin.com

CONNECT WITH US AT:

Harlequin.com/Community

 Facebook.com/HarlequinBooks

 Twitter.com/HarlequinBooks

 Instagram.com/HarlequinBooks

 Pinterest.com/HarlequinBooks

ReaderService.com

**ROMANCE WHEN
YOU NEED IT**

HSOCIAL2017